Midnight's Choice

Also by Kate Thompson in Red Fox

Switchers

Wild Blood

The Missing Link

Only Human

The Beguilers

KATE THOMPSON

Midnight's Choice

RED FOX

For Oisin

A Red Fox Book

Published by Random House Children's Books
20 Vauxhall Bridge Road, London SW1V 2SA

A division of The Random House Group Limited
London Melbourne Sydney Auckland
Johannesburg and agencies throughout the world

First published in Great Britain by
The Bodley Head Children's Books 1998

This Red Fox edition 2001

3 5 7 9 10 8 6 4 2

Printed and bound in Great Britain by
Bookmarque Ltd, Croydon, Surrey

Papers used by The Random House Group are natural, recyclable products
made from wood grown in sustainable forests. The manufacturing
processes conform to the environmental regulations
of the country of origin.

The Random House Group Limited Reg. No. 9540009

www.randomhouse.co.uk

ISBN 0 09 941765 0

CHAPTER ONE

The white rat watched as the two golden birds rose up into the night sky and disappeared from view. A few minutes ago, one of them had been his owner, Tess. Then she had seen the other bird on the tree outside her window, and she had shimmered, changed, and flown away. For a moment or two the rat remained still, staring into the empty darkness in perplexity, then he twitched his whiskers, washed his nose with his paws and jumped back on to his exercise wheel.

As she soared up high above the park, Tess had no thought of what she had left behind her. In her young life, she had used her secret ability to Switch to experience many different forms of animal life, but she had never been a phoenix before. All her attention was absorbed by this new and exhilarating experience, and until she had become comfortable with it, she could think of nothing else.

She followed the other bird faithfully as he rose through the night sky, higher and higher. Each sweep of her golden wings seemed effortless, and propelled her so far that she felt almost weightless. Behind her, the long sweeping tail seemed to have no more substance than the tail of a comet. It was as though the nature of the bird was to rise upwards; gravity had scarcely any power over it at all.

Up and up the two of them flew, not slowing until they had risen well clear of the city's sulphurous halo and into the crisp, cool air beyond. Then the three-toed phoenix began to drift upwards in a more leisurely way and eventually came to a halt. Tess slowed down and began to hover beside her friend, using her wings to tread the air as a swimmer treads water. But when she looked at him, she noticed that he wasn't using his wings. He was merely sitting on the air, floating without any effort at all. With slight apprehension, she followed suit and stilled her wings. It worked. The two of them floated there, weightless as clouds, looking down on the city of Dublin below.

Back in Tess's bedroom, the white rat's wheel was spinning so fast that its bearings were getting hot. He didn't understand what had occurred when Tess had Switched and taken flight but it excited him, and the only way he had of expressing that excitement was in movement. So he ran and ran, the bars of the wheel becoming blurred as they passed beneath his racing feet, again and again and again.

A faint breeze moved the curtain and reached the rat's cage. He paused in his stride, then stopped so abruptly that the flying wheel carried him right round inside it three times before it fell to swinging him back and forth and finally came to rest. The white rat was frozen to the spot, every nerve on edge as he strained his senses to understand what that mysterious breeze had brought with it. He waited, and was just about to return to his futile travels when the message came again. There was no mistaking it this time. Somewhere in the city streets, someone or something was sending out a call which Algernon had no power to resist. He hurled himself against the side of the cage, scrabbling with his paws and biting the bars. When this failed he began to dig frantically against the metal floor, throwing food and sawdust and water in all directions in his desperation to escape. But the cage was too well made. The message grew weaker until at last the white rat resigned himself and curled up, exhausted, among the disordered bedding in the corner.

Once Tess had become accustomed to the strange sensation of floating, she turned her attention to her friend. Everything had happened so quickly that she hadn't even greeted him yet; not properly, anyway. There was so much she wanted to know, so much news to catch up on. There was no need for them to recount their adventures in the Arctic when they had fought the dreadful krools; nor was there any need to remember the awful moment when Kevin had Switched just a moment too late and got caught by the flying napalm. The last time she had seen him he had been a small bird, burning, tumbling into the flaming forest below, and there had seemed no possibility of hope.

She could understand the leap of imagination that had enabled him to escape by turning into a phoenix and rising again from his own ashes, but a lot of time had gone by since then and she was impatient to know where he had been and what he had done.

She turned to look at him, but when she caught sight of his golden eyes, all her questions suddenly seemed to be without meaning. Her mind stilled and became peaceful, merging into his in a kind of featureless calm. All at once, Tess felt that she knew all there was to know about the nature of the phoenix. It was ageless, timeless, the essence of all that was pure and beyond the reach of mortal concerns.

Far below, the life of the city continued despite the lateness of the hour. The last buses returned to the station and parked; taxis picked up party-goers and brought them home; lovers stretched the evening on into the small hours, strolling slowly home. Beneath the roofs, nurses worked night-shifts, presses rolled with the morning's newspapers, babies and small children woke and cried, bringing their parents groggily from bed. And still further down, in their own subsystem of homes and highways, hundreds of thousands of city rats were awake and going about their business. From her great height, Tess perceived it all happening. It was her city, her home, and yet she was so detached from it that she might as well have been looking down on an ants' nest. She sank into the ecstasy of the experience and all her cares melted away.

When Tess returned to her bedroom shortly before dawn and resumed her human form, the sense of joyousness remained with her. It was as though all the worries of the last few months had vanished and been replaced by a calm certainty that the future was assured. The choice of the final form that she would have to take when she reached her fifteenth birthday seemed to have been made for her.

Nothing that she had ever been before could

compare with the serene, weightless existence of the phoenix, and she could not imagine ever wanting to be anything else. Already she was beginning to miss it.

Although she wasn't particularly tired, Tess got into her pyjamas and snatched a couple of hours' sleep before breakfast. So it wasn't until her father woke her and she began to get into her school uniform that she noticed the state of the white rat's cage. There was always a certain amount of clearing up to be done there in the mornings, but Tess had never seen anything like this before. The water bowl had been knocked over and the floor was a mess of soggy food and sawdust. The top of the chest of drawers where the cage stood and the carpet underneath it were both littered with debris that the rat's scrabbling feet had thrown out, and the shredded paper of his bedding had been pulled out of the nest-box and slung over the wheel like festive streamers.

'What on earth have you been up to, Algernon?' said Tess.

In reply, the white rat hopped into the wheel for a morning stroll, but before he had done two turns the paper strips caught up in the axle and jammed it.

Tess tried to speak to him in the visual language of the rats that she had learnt during her adventures with Kevin.

'Sunflower seeds and shavings all over the place, huh? White rat digging, huh? White rat angry, huh?'

Algernon twitched his nose in bewilderment. Tess finished dressing, then took him out of the cage and put him on the floor while she sorted out the mess.

5

He was his usual timid self, never straying far from Tess's feet and investigating her school bag with the utmost care, as though something large and aggressive might leap out of it and grab him. By the time she had emptied the contents of the cage into a plastic bag and replaced it with fresh food and bedding, he was standing up against Tess's shoe, sniffing the air above him and longing to get back home.

'Tess!' came her mother's voice from the kitchen.

'I'm coming,' she called back, releasing the wheel from its bearings and starting to unwind the tangled paper. It broke in her fingers every time she tried to pull it clear of the wheel, and looked like taking a lot longer to unravel than she had expected.

'Tess!'

'Yes!'

'Your breakfast is ready!'

'All right, all right, I'm coming!' Irritation was apparent in her voice, and she felt disgusted with herself, aware of how rapidly the righteous mood of a few hours ago had passed. She made one more attempt to free the wheel's axle, then threw it down in disgust.

'Cage with no wheel in it,' she said to Algernon in Rat as she picked him up from the floor, a little roughly.

'Huh?' said Algernon. He loved his wheel. Apart from eating and sleeping, it was the only pleasure he had in life. But Tess had one eye on the racing clock and was growing angrier by the minute.

'White rat with no brain,' she said. 'White rat with hairless baby rats in nest.' She shoved him into the cage and closed the door.

'Huh?' he said again. 'Huh?'

Tess ignored him. She tied a knot in the top of the

6

plastic bag and turned her mind to what she was likely to need in school that day. They would be playing camogie: that would mean helmet and hurley . . .

'Tess! You're going to be late!'

She ran downstairs and snatched a hasty breakfast, then raced for the bus. As it brought her through the streets of the city she looked up into the sky, hoping to catch a glint of gold; some sign that it hadn't all been a foolish dream. Clouds had gathered since the early hours, and from time to time a ray of sunshine broke through them, but she knew that it had nothing to do with the phoenix.

The phoenix. As she thought about him, and about the time they had spent up there above the city, Tess realised that, although the bird undoubtedly was Kevin, it wasn't the friend she had known. In all their previous adventures together, no matter what form they had taken, they would recognise each other instantly. Rats, goats, dolphins, even mammoths and dragons had not served to disguise the individuality of the person who dwelt within them. But the more Tess thought about it, the harder she found it to identify the Kevin she knew and loved with that lofty, ethereal bird. When she remembered the way it had felt to be with him, the sense of joyous detachment and freedom, she longed to be back there again, away from the smoggy trundling of the traffic and the dreary day ahead. But it was, she realised, because of the delight of the phoenix nature and not because of any sense of companionship. The joy of that experience ought to be sustaining her, but instead it was being nudged aside by doubt. Where was Kevin? Where was all the rest of him, the mischievousness and the moodiness and the flash of anger that came to his eyes? There was no sign of any of those things in the phoenix. It was like some kind of divine being, capable of nothing except existing; just radiating light and goodness.

Her mind wandered and returned to the problem of Algernon and his unusual behaviour. When she remembered how unkind she had been to him, she was sorry. Poor creature. He wasn't very smart, it was true, but he had the sweetest temperament imaginable. He was incapable of an unkind thought. How could she have been so cruel to him?

She closed her eyes and leant her head on the back of the seat. Taking a deep breath, she tried to think herself into the mood of perfect understanding that the form of the phoenix had given her the night before. But the only revelation she received was that she had, after all, forgotten her helmet and her hurley. She was going to be in big trouble.

CHAPTER TWO

Tess had a lousy day at school, and not only because she had forgotten her camogie kit. Her mind refused to apply itself to the work in hand, and at every opportunity she sank into euphoric day-dream memories of the previous night. Only when she was ticked off by one of the teachers did she return her attention to the present. Her class-mates found her even more strange and dreamy than usual, and one or two of the more cynical ones took the opportunity to tease her.

'Look at Madam Tess with her head in the clouds.'

'Oh. Better than the rest of us, that one. Wouldn't bother trying to communicate with her.'

'You'd need to be on your knees to do that.'

'You'd need a priest.'

'Come on, exalted one, hear us, we pray.'

'Oh, stuff it, will you?' she said at last.

'Stuff it, stuff it. Hear ye, the almighty one has spoken. We must stuff it, one and all.'

Tess moved away, but the harsh laughter continued to ring in her ears long after the other girls had forgotten the incident. She knew that they could never understand what she was going through, but their reaction made her uneasy all the same. Glorious as it was, the phoenix experience seemed to be increasing her sense of loneliness and isolation.

At home that evening, she went straight up to her room. The white rat popped his head out of the nest box where he had been sleeping away a dull day. He looked for his wheel, still bewildered by the change in his circumstances, then stood up against the bars of the cage, whiskers twitching, pink eyes peering around ineffectually for Tess.

She opened the cage door and lifted him out. He fitted snugly into the crook of her arm as she stroked his sleek coat and apologised to him for her impatience that morning.

'Poor Algernon. It wasn't your fault, was it?' Her mind drifted back to the skies above the city and she turned to the window. It was January and already dark, but she hadn't drawn her curtains yet. Although she could see nothing beyond the black squares of the glass, she knew that somewhere out there the phoenix was waiting for her. It would be another year before her fifteenth birthday, another year before she had to decide once and for all what form the rest of her life would take. But what was there to say that she couldn't make that decision sooner? Why shouldn't she make it tonight, if she wanted to? She could be free of school and home and all those human concerns that dragged at her existence. She could be out there with her friend and not a worry in the world. Once again the memory of the night before crept back, filling her with that glorious sense of lightness and well-being.

'Tess?'

Tess jumped. Her mother was standing in the doorway. 'Your tea is ready. Are you all right?'

'Yes. Just day-dreaming.'

'Anything wrong?'

'No. Nothing at all.' Tess stood up and slipped Algernon back into his cage, then followed her mother down the stairs.

As soon as she had finished her tea, Tess started on her homework, but when her father came home two hours later she was still struggling with a simple history project, unable to make her wandering mind concentrate. She put it away unfinished and joined her parents for dinner, the one meal of the day when they all sat down together.

The meal seemed to take for ever. Tess pushed her food around the plate and sighed a lot. Her father tried to chivvy the conversation along but it was a thankless task. As soon as she could, Tess made for the peace and quiet of her own room and settled herself to wait; she could do nothing safely until her parents were asleep. She could hear their quiet voices in the room below, and she wondered if they were talking about her, discussing her uncharacteristic loss of appetite or her dreamy mood. She wished, as she had done many times before, that she was not the only child, that she had sisters or brothers to share the responsibility with her.

The night was cold and windy, but Tess opened the window anyway and peered out. The darkness above the park was muddied by the street-lights, whose orange radiance leaked upwards like escaping heat. But beyond it, Tess could just make out a few faint stars appearing and disappearing as heavy clouds moved across the sky. As she watched, it seemed to her that one of them was a little brighter than the others, and golden in colour. She fixed her eyes on it, unsure whether it was drawing closer or whether her imagination was playing tricks. The star seemed to blink and turn. Was it moving? Did it have a tail which streamed out behind it, even a short way?

Tess's concentration was abruptly broken by a loud scratching noise from Algernon's cage. She turned and saw him trying to burrow into the corner where his wheel had been, throwing sawdust all over the cage and out through the bars.

'Poor old Algernon,' said Tess and then, in Rat, 'Wheel, huh?'

Algernon made no reply, but turned his attention to another corner of the cage and continued to scrabble away desperately. It was uncharacteristic behaviour, and it worried Tess. She picked up the wheel and began again to unravel the wound-up paper from around the axle. She had done most of the work that morning, and it didn't take long to free it and clear the last few shreds which were draped between the bars.

'Here you go, Algie. Is this what you want?' Tess opened the hatch in the top of the cage and reached in with the wheel in her hand. Before she could react, before she could even blink, Algernon had run up the bars of the cage, out through the hatch, and down Tess's legs to the floor. Tess stared at him in amazement. She had never seen him behave like that before. Something must have happened to him. His timidity was gone, and instead of bumbling round short-sightedly he was scuttling into the corners of the room and scratching at the carpet with his claws.

Quickly, Tess refitted the wheel and checked that it was spinning freely. Then she tidied up the floor of the cage, picked the stray shavings out of the food-bowl, and replaced the dirty water with fresh from the tap.

By this time Algernon was at the door, poking his paws into the narrow gap beneath it and gnawing at the wood with his teeth. When Tess reached down to pick him up, he jumped in fright, as though he had been taken by surprise. He had never done that before, either. He wriggled and squirmed as she pushed him through the small door of the cage, and threw himself against it when she closed it. Tess hoped it was the loss of the wheel that had upset him, and that once he found it back in its place he would settle himself down. His behaviour disturbed her more than she liked to admit, and she wondered if she should take him to the vet.

'White rat in pain, huh?' she said to him. 'White rat afraid of sore head? Sore belly?'

Algernon paused in his restless scurrying and looked at her. 'White rat go,' he said, his thought images dim and poorly formed. 'White rat go under city.'

His pictures of the rats' underground system were whimsy, like a young child's drawing of a fairy-tale land. But it was the first time he had used that image, or even given any intimation that he knew such a place existed.

'Brown rats in tunnels,' said Tess. 'Brown rats tough, fierce, biting white rat.'

'White rat go,' said Algernon stubbornly, his restlessness returning. 'White rat go, white rat go, white

13

rat go.' He began to chew with his yellow teeth at the bars of the cage.

Tess sighed. 'Teeth worn down,' she said to him. 'Sunflower seeds won't open, white rat hungry.'

Algernon took no notice whatsoever. Tess returned to the window, but it was impossible for her to relax with the sound of Algernon chewing and scratching and rushing around his cage. Eventually she picked up a book and went downstairs, hoping that he would settle down in her absence. If he was still the same way tomorrow she could bring him to the vet.

Her parents were glad to see her coming down, and her father made room for her on the sofa beside him.

'Everything all right?' he said.

'Just Algernon. He's a bit restless. It's not like him.'

'I expect he needs a pal,' said her mother. 'What about getting another one?'

'As long as it's not female,' said her father. 'There's enough rats in the world as it is without breeding more of them.'

Tess laughed, reassured. The TV programme was humorous, the room was warm, and she had no premonition at all of the dramatic changes that were about to come into her life.

When the evening film was over, Tess brought an apple upstairs to share with Algernon as a bed-time treat. The rat however, had other things on his mind. The room was cold when Tess came into it, and the first thing she did was to go across and close the window. There was no sign of the phoenix beyond it, and she turned her attention to Algernon. He was upside down, hanging by his paws to the wire roof and gnawing on the metal clasp which kept the

14

roof hatch secure. The water bowl had been knocked over again, and almost the entire contents of the cage had been hurled through the bars, littering up the room in a wide circle around the cage. Tess groaned and fought down a desire to punish the white rat. He was already disturbed enough, and scaring him further would not accomplish anything. Far better to try and find out what the problem was.

'Apple, huh?' she said.

In reply, Algernon dropped from the top of the cage, twisting in mid-air so that he landed on his feet, then proceeded to perform the most extraordinary feat of rodent gymnastics, leaping up the sides of the cage, across the roof and down to the floor again in a dizzying sequence of somersaults.

'White rat go, white rat go, white rat go,' he repeated as he swung wildly around.

Tess began to realise that the situation was much more serious than she had thought. It was clear now that the problem wasn't just going to disappear and there was no sense in trying to ignore it. Where did Algernon want to go, and why? She turned his repetitive visual statement into a question and, in reply, Algernon sent a most extraordinary image into her mind.

It was a little like the visual name the city rats had given to Kevin, a gruesome mixture of rat and a rat's conception of a boy. But this new image was vaguer, and tied up with other images as well; wolves perhaps, and bats, all in darkness. Strangest thing of all, and the most disturbing thing to Tess's human mind, was that this being was calling. It was calling for all the rats in the city to come towards it, and the reason for Algernon's behaviour was suddenly crystal clear. For Tess could tell without any doubt that if

she had been a rat at that moment, she would have
had no resistance whatsoever to that call.

CHAPTER THREE

Tess sat on the windowsill and stared out into the darkness, longing for the phoenix to come. Behind her, Algernon was still rattling against the sides of his cage, his anxiety growing into a kind of dementia as he found that all his efforts were useless. Tess kept her mind firmly closed to his pathetic babbling. The weird communication that she had tuned into with her rat mind disturbed her a great deal and she knew that she was turning her back on the problem. But the lure of the phoenix was too strong.

Her parents' door eventually closed, and in a surprisingly short time she heard her father's regular snores coming through the wall. There was still no sign of the golden creature, but as she looked out into the darkness, Tess realised that this didn't matter. She could still re-live the experience on her own. The wonder of being a phoenix had nothing to do with companionship. It was beyond companionship; beyond all worldly attachments.

She was just on the point of deciding to Switch when something happened which made her change her mind. In a last, desperate attempt to break free, Algernon hurled himself at the door of the cage with such force that it sprang open and he found himself sliding over the edge of the chest of drawers and falling towards the floor. Tess caught sight of him as he fell, but before she could get to him he had landed, picked himself up, and was racing towards the corner of the room.

Tess followed, irritated by the delay but concerned as well. Despite Algernon's limitations as a companion, she was fond of him and she would have hated to see him coming to any harm.

There was no fireplace in Tess's room but there had been one, long ago, and the chimney-breast ran up one wall. Beside it was a redundant corner, about the size of a wardrobe, and Tess had helped her father to put doors across it when they first moved in. She kept her clothes there, hanging from an old broom handle, and beneath them her shoes and boots were arranged on the floor.

Algernon ran straight towards this cupboard as though he knew exactly where he was going. Tess and her father had never got around to fixing bolts on to the doors, and they always stood slightly open. Algernon nosed through the gap and disappeared among the footwear. Tess followed and pulled the doors wide open, just in time to see the rat's pink tail disappearing down a tiny gap between the floor-boards and the wall of the chimney-breast. There was only one way to follow him. Switching had become so much a part of Tess's nature that she no longer had to think about it. She didn't even stand still but, in one fluid movement, changed into a brown rat and went slithering down the hole in hot pursuit.

Beneath the floor and behind the walls, a maze of old rat passage-ways ran through the house. Tess hadn't known they were there, but she might have guessed. All old houses are riddled with rat-runs, even if they aren't in current use.

Despite Tess's speed, Algernon had already disappeared behind the first of the joists which ran beneath the floorboards. But to her surprise, Tess realised that she didn't need to follow him. Her rat mind had picked up on the command from the mysterious stranger, and there was no doubt that she and Algernon were heading in the same direction.

She scuttled down through the walls of the house, between the courses of bricks, until she came into a long, rat-made conduit which connected with the drains. At the end of that, she caught a glimpse of Algernon's tail as he turned a bend in a pipe. She accelerated, and after a few more twists and turns she found that she was gaining on him. Before long she had caught up, but when she tried to communicate with him, he ignored her, his mind fixed exclusively on the unknown destination ahead.

The most direct way of following the call led the two rats across the city by way of drains and under-floor passages. Tess was surprised by Algernon's speed and agility, and also by his apparent lack of fear. She realised as she ran beside him that this was what he had been deprived of as he grew up in his artificial environment. It was no surprise that he was dull-witted and inarticulate, since he had missed out on the rats' basic education in life. But all that was changing now. Who could tell how much his intelligence might increase, provided he could avoid the common pitfalls of city rats and stay alive long enough to learn his way around.

One of these hazards, poison, was very much in evidence in several of the gardens they had to pass through. Tess was on guard, but Algernon was far too preoccupied to be diverted by food, no matter how enticing it smelled. Where cats were concerned, however, his single-mindedness was a considerable handicap and, on two separate occasions, Tess had to rescue him; once by steering him away from the waiting jaws of a large tom, and once by charging a cat that was just about to grab him from behind. The cat was so surprised by Tess's aggression that she turned tail and fled, and by the time she had recovered herself, the two rats were long gone.

The rest of the journey was safer. When they joined the sewers, Algernon proved to be an excellent swimmer, and his regular exercise on the wheel had made him fit enough to cope with the slippery exertions of climbing back out of them. By the time they surfaced, in order to cross a small open square, he was a lot less white than he had been, but still not as camouflaged as Tess would have liked him to be. Because what she feared most for him had yet to be encountered, and that was the reaction of the other rats. She was not surprised that they hadn't come across any before now, because she was working on the assumption that all the others within range of the strange call had got a long head start on them. They were stragglers, she and Algernon, bringing up the rear. But she knew that before long they would be getting close to their destination, close to the moment of truth.

They dropped back into the underworld by means

of a hole in the ground beneath the cover of bushes in a corner of the tiny park. Tess called to Algernon again, warning him to take his time and watch out for cats, but when she opened her mind for his reply she caught nothing but a babble of rat images. They were close. Above them, they could hear the deep rumble of a car passing along a street. A moment later they were on the other side and, surprisingly, beginning to climb.

Abruptly, Algernon stopped. He was ahead of Tess and blocking the narrow passage which ran higgledy piggledy through a foundation wall between detached houses. She couldn't see beyond him, but she could hear the restless rustling of a great gathering of rats. Impatiently, Tess squeezed her way in beside Algernon, whose fluid body seemed to elongate as he made room for her in the narrow space. They were looking into the kitchen of a vacant house. Tess held her breath, astonished by what she was seeing. There were rats of all shapes and sizes: rats with grey coats, brown coats, black coats, sleek rats and mangy rats, thin rats and fat ones, all milling around in an aimless fashion. The dim light on their moving backs made Tess think of water, rippling and flowing. The kitchen was flooded with rats.

Her first concern was for Algernon. The hole in the wall where they were standing was about two feet from the ground. It would be easy to slip down the wall on to the floor, but not so easy to climb back up if there was trouble down there. A rat could scale that height in a flash, but not without a run-up. Already a few twitching noses were beginning to turn and look with curiosity at the two newcomers. Tess tried to pick up on the reactions, but the images she received were the visual equivalent of a roar in a football stadium – it was impossible to pick out any individual communication. She scanned the crowd, hoping to find someone she knew, but there was no one she recognised. She hesitated, and beside her Algernon was hesitating too. Whatever certainty had brought him here was severely weakened by the sight of so many rough and street-wise relatives.

Their decision was made for them. Without warning, another group of latecomers arrived in the passage behind them and, in their urgency to obey the call, they crowded forward relentlessly, pushing Tess and Algernon out of the hole in the wall and down into the restless mob below. Tess scrabbled through the crowd, desperate to stay close to Algernon and defend him against attack, but to her relief it proved unnecessary. The other rats grudgingly made space for him on the floor. Those closest to him inspected him curiously, but none had time or energy for aggression. All minds were firmly fixed on the powerful call that had brought them together.

Tess tuned into it as accurately as she could. It was a strange feeling, being drawn to something she could neither see nor hear, but which exerted such a powerful attraction on the rat part of her mind. It wasn't an active call; none of the rats was being asked to do anything except be there. It was as though they had been drawn by some sort of magnetism and were now held within its field of force, powerless to move away.

When she looked round, Tess saw Algernon struggling across the backs of the other rats towards the opposite side of the room. She tried to call him, aware that walking on another rat's back without permission is extremely bad manners. But if he heard her at all, he ignored her and carried on, oblivious to the warning clouts and nips that the other rats were giving him. Tess bared her teeth in exasperation and followed. There is no equivalent of an apology in the rat language; instead, Tess tried to convey a sense of urgency to the rats whose backs she crossed. It was of little use, however, since all but the eldest and wisest rats in the gathering were feeling a similar sense of urgency and had little patience with shovers. By the time Tess caught up with Algernon on the other side of the room, she was covered in little cuts and bruises and thoroughly fed up.

Algernon was scratched and bitten too, but he didn't seem to care. He was wriggling into a small hole that had been chewed in the bottom of the door which led into the hall. Tess followed. This narrow space was full of limp cardboard boxes and dusty trunks, long since abandoned. Rats were packed into every available space, level upon level of them, like the audience at a mega pop concert. A flight of stairs ran down from the floor above, and Tess noticed something which filled her rat mind with wry amusement. On the top step a cat was sitting, its face turned away in silent uninterest, as though it had no idea that it was surrounded by its worst enemy. Tess knew that the nonchalance was feigned, that beneath its smug exterior that cat was absolutely terrified. It was another measure of the single-mindedness of the gathered rats that they didn't set upon the poor creature and tear it to shreds. Despite herself, Tess hoped that they wouldn't change their minds.

Ahead of her, Algernon was slithering through the gathering again, over and under and around, any way that he could see of getting across the room. Tess followed, steeling herself against another series of bites and blows. From time to time she looked around her, hoping to catch a glimpse of friends from the past; Long Nose, perhaps, or Stuck Six Days in a Gutter Pipe. but she had no luck. They could have been anywhere. There was no way for Tess to tell how many rats had gathered, or if any were exempt from the call.

Algernon scuttled along beside the wall and Tess followed, determined to try and hold him still by force if once she managed to catch up with him. But as they slipped through the open door into the front room, a new message began on the stranger's mental wavelength. It was electrifying. Every rat in the place sprang to attention, some sitting up on their tails or standing on their hind legs in an effort to understand.

Tess was no less attentive than the others. The images coming into her mind were quite clear. The rats were to search beneath the city for a certain type of large, stone container. Some of these structures would be open to the human world, in huge basement rooms where they were regularly visited. Others would be buried in the ground where no humans could reach, and these were the kind that the rats had to go and find. If and when they succeeded they were to return and report.

That was all. As abruptly as it had started, the communication ended, and for a moment there was a profound silence. Then the visual babble began again, becoming pandemonium as a hundred thousand rats began to react. Tess resisted the temptation to join the confusion and looked round. Rats were pouring out of the room as though someone had let the plug out. She caught a glimpse of Algernon disappearing into a hole, like a piece of white paper being swept by the current into a drain, and a moment later she was alone.

CHAPTER FOUR

About a mile away, Jeff Maloney, the head keeper of Dublin Zoo, was being woken from a deep sleep by the phone. His irritation at being disturbed was worsened by the fact that he had only just got to sleep, following a long evening trying, unsuccessfully, to save a new-born calf in the pet section. Even now it was the first thought that came to his mind. The irony of it. The zoo had successfully bred hippos, elephants and rhinos, but when it came to a common Jersey cow, they had been powerless to save the calf.

As he crossed the sitting room, Jeff tripped over a dog first, and then a chair. He was swearing by the time he reached the light-switch, but it was nothing compared to the torrent of abuse that he let loose when the phone stopped ringing the instant before he reached it.

Tess stood in the middle of the floor and tried to

gather her thoughts. She sent out a few half-hearted calls towards Algernon and her other rat friends, but if any rat picked them up he or she was far too preoccupied to respond. It was all so confusing, and Tess's rat mind hadn't much space for rational thought. For a few moments she scuttled around the empty house with the vague idea of finding something to eat in order to calm her nerves. At the top of the stairs, the cat was still frozen in the same position, even though all the other rats were gone. Tess knew that the poor creature would climb walls rather than go in there again.

Think; she needed to think. Slipping back into the third of the rooms, she Switched back into human form. The smell of rats was strong, even to a human being's weak sense of smell. Tess wondered how she would feel if she opened the door one day and found her own house as full of rats as this one had been. Her parents would call in pest control; the house would be evacuated – perhaps the whole street. But no matter how hard people tried, they would never get rid of the rats in the city. There would still be rats there long after the human race had died out or moved elsewhere.

Tess shivered. She was still wearing her school uniform, but without a cardigan or a jacket. She was wasting time. As soon as she put her human mind to the problem which faced her she began to see her way forward. The image of the person that had called was still confused, but of two things she was sure. He was a boy, and he was a Switcher. The realisation brought a sense of excitement with it, because Kevin had told her that all Switchers must meet with another to pass on their knowledge. She had often wondered since whether this was true and, if so, when she would encounter this new friend. Now it seemed that the time had come. The only problem was that she still had to find him.

She concentrated hard, trying to remember how it had felt to her as a rat when the message had come through so strongly. Where, exactly, had it come from? Somewhere above, she realised, and behind her as she stood now. She turned round. Yes, that way. Not directly above, but ahead of her now; a house across the street perhaps?

Jeff Maloney was just getting comfortable in bed when the phone rang again. For a few seconds he hesitated, then decided not to ignore it. He took a different route across the sitting room this time, but unfortunately the dog had also decided to change location, and once again there was an outraged yelp as Jeff's foot came into contact.

This time he went straight for the phone, fumbling in the darkness for the receiver.

'Hello?'

'Hello. Jeff Maloney?'

'Speaking.'

'Garda barracks here. We have a report of an unusual bird at the edge of the Phoenix Park. We were wondering whether you had lost any.'

Jeff had visions of blundering around with nets in the night. It wouldn't be the first time such a thing had happened. 'What sort of bird?'

'I'll hand you over to the witness, hold on.'

There was a crackle, and then a sort of knocking sound, as though the receiver at the other end had been dropped on the floor. At last a rather drunken voice came on to the line.

'Hello?'

'Hello.'

'Hello?'

'Hello. Jeff Maloney here. You've seen an unusual bird?'

'By God, I have. Never saw anything like it. It must be one of your lads, come out of the zoo. I never saw anything like it.'

'Can you describe it to me?'

'It was golden, pure golden. I never saw anything like it.'

Jeff gritted his teeth, convinced that he was dealing with a hallucination. It wouldn't have been the first time that had happened, either. 'Can you tell me any more?' he said.

'I've never seen anything like it. It had . . . sort of . . . long tail feathers, hanging down. And it was golden.'

'Probably a hen pheasant,' said Jeff. 'We quite often see them in the park at this time of year. Was it sitting in a tree?'

'It was, by God, but it wasn't a pheasant, no way. It was golden, pure golden, I've never seen anything like it.'

Jeff sighed. 'A trick of the light, I'd imagine,' he said, as kindly as he could. 'Those street lights can have a strange effect sometimes.'

'Well, you can say what you like,' said the voice on the other end of the line, 'but that was no pheasant, hen or cock. I've–'

' – never seen anything like it, I know,' said Jeff, his patience finally deserting him. 'I appreciate your calling, and I'll check it out first thing in the morning on my way to work.'

'It'll be your loss if it's gone by then,' said the voice.

'It'll be my loss if I don't get a bit of sleep tonight, too. Goodnight, and thank you for your information.'

As he put down the receiver, Jeff heard the dog shuffling into the corner, well out of range.

The best way for Tess to get out of the empty house was to become a rat again. She made her way out by using a series of passages and air vents, then checked carefully up and down before leaving cover.

The street meant nothing to her. It was like dozens of others in the area, made up of two-storey brick-built houses dating from the fifties and early sixties. For some reason, she had thought that she would recognise the house where the Switcher was living as soon as she saw it, but now that she was out in the open, one house looked pretty much like the next.

A car came slowly down the street and Tess instinctively slipped into the damp and oily gutter, sheltering behind the wheel of a parked van until the coast was clear. When she came out from behind the wheel, it was in the shape of a small mongrel dog. She had often used this form when a certain type of investigation was needed.

It was no use, though. She patrolled the length of the street in both directions, catching every available scent from the sleeping households, but there was nothing out of the ordinary. She had hoped for some lingering residue of the Switcher's ability, a variety of animal smells coming from one of the houses perhaps, or one of an unusual nature. But apart from the still pervasive smell of rats, there was nothing out of the ordinary at all. The dog's nose couldn't help.

She craned her neck to look at the upstairs windows. Presumably, whoever had called the rats was still awake, which probably meant a light on somewhere. But the only lighted windows were in a house at the end of the street, and the voices which could be heard coming from it were of people much older than Switchers could be.

Tess considered changing into something smaller and taking a look around the inside of a few of the houses, but her instinct told her it was beginning to get late. She remembered the phoenix with longing, and became aware of the time she was wasting by trotting up and down the empty street. There would be other nights for investigating; all she needed to do was to find out where she was and she could come back any time. So she trotted along until she found the sign on the wall which told her the name of the street. To her dog mind it meant nothing, just a white square with bits of black stuck on it, like the bits of cars which were at her eye level and which had to be avoided if they were moving.

Tess looked along the street. There was no sign of anyone around but she still felt too exposed to Switch. The nearby houses had tiny front gardens with low walls; no cover at all. The best place she could find was the pavement between a transit van and the windowless corner wall of the end house. She slipped in there and sat down close to the kerb. Then, with a last glance around her, she Switched. She waited for a minute or two, then got up and strolled back to look at the street-name. There was still no sign of anyone awake. She had been lucky.

Back in bed once again, Jeff Maloney found that he couldn't sleep. He lay on his back first, then each side in turn, and finally on his stomach, but he just couldn't get comfortable. He thought about his last girlfriend and about his next one, whom he hadn't yet met but who would be perfect in every way when he did. He thought about what he would do on his day off, and what he would do in his summer holidays, but nothing worked. Every time he got comfortably absorbed in his thoughts, the slightly slurred voice returned to his mind: 'It'll be your loss if it's gone by then.'

Eventually, with a sigh of exasperation, he threw back the covers and sat up on the edge of the bed. 'I should have been an accountant,' he said to himself.

It was as well that Tess, in the shape of a pigeon, was able to cross the city faster than Jeff Maloney could cross the park. At the time he was visiting the barracks and getting the exact location of the alleged sighting, Tess was joining the three-toed phoenix on the branch of the tree outside her window. But the distant glimpse that the zoo-keeper got of two flecks of gold rising into the night sky was enough to rouse his curiosity.

CHAPTER FIVE

The following morning, when Tess's father went into her room to wake her, he found her bed empty. As he looked round, his heart filled with anxiety, he noticed that Algernon's cage was empty too.

'Tess?' he called, checking the bathroom and going on down the stairs. 'Tess, where are you?'

'What's wrong?' called her mother from the bedroom.

'Can't find Tess. Don't worry, she can't be far away.'

She wasn't. He saw her as soon as he drew the curtains in the kitchen, out in the back garden on her hands and knees.

He opened the window. 'What on earth are you doing out there, Tess? You gave me the fright of my life.'

Tess looked up, revealing a nasty-looking graze on her cheek and another above her nose. 'I was looking for Algernon,' she said. 'I brought him out for some exercise this morning and he's disappeared.'

It was the only excuse she could think of. She had arrived back from the second spell of being a phoenix just a few minutes ago, and realised that she had no way of getting into the house. Her window was closed, and it would take too long to find her way into the right system of underground passages if she tried to get in as a rat. There hadn't been much time to think.

'But it's hardly even light yet,' said her father. 'Why on earth did you get up so early? And what's happened to your face?'

Tess's mother, always put on edge by the slightest sign of strange behaviour, joined her husband at the window.

'What have you done to yourself?'

For a moment Tess had no idea what they were talking about. She couldn't recall having done anything to her face. Just in time she remembered the bites and scratches she had received from the other rats when she was following Algernon a few hours ago. There were probably a lot more scrapes and bruises hidden by her uniform. She thought quickly.

'I was feeling around in the bushes there,' she said, pointing to a shady corner where several well-established shrubs were growing. 'Have I cut myself?'

'You certainly have,' said her mother. 'Come in, now, and let me have a look.'

'But what about Algernon?'

'You'll have to worry about him later. He can't be far away.'

Tess felt in her pocket. 'You'll have to let me in,' she said. 'I left my key in my coat.'

As her mother fussed over her face, Tess slipped

back into the warm, euphoric memory of the phoenix nature that she had abandoned just a few minutes before. She scarcely felt the antiseptic on the wounds, barely heard her mother saying, 'They're not as bad as they look. Just scratches.' She was floating again, high above it all, filled with brightness and peace.

'Wakey, wakey.'

'Hmm?'

Her father put a plate of scrambled eggs on toast in front of her on the table. Tess's stomach rose in protest, and she wondered why it was that the nightly sessions as a phoenix made her lose her appetite. She played with the scrambled egg but ate no more than a couple of mouthfuls.

'Are you worried about something?' her mother asked.

'Just Algernon. I think I'll have another look around outside.'

'No. You get yourself ready for school. I'll have a good look for him after you've gone. He can't be far away.'

That day was even worse than the one before. Tess had not slept at all during the night, and although the phoenix mood was invigorating and relaxing, she could only sustain its memory for short periods of time. When it was gone she was exhausted and depressed, and felt weak from lack of food. She was worried about what was happening with the rats as well, and between her various preoccupations found no energy or attention for her school work. On two occasions she narrowly avoided detention, and she promised herself that she would take a nap when she got home before she made any decisions about what she was going to do next.

But as the bus passed through Phibsboro that evening, she suddenly recognised the area of streets where she and the other rats had ended up the previous night. Before she had time to think, she had made her way to the front of the bus, and at the next stop she got off.

It would make her late home. Were other girls of her age never late home? Did they never make independent decisions to call on some friend or go into town for a coffee? Would her mother believe her if she used an excuse like that? 'I went to listen to Catriona's new R.E.M. tape, Mum.' Or, 'I felt like walking a bit of the way home.' Why shouldn't she? She was fourteen, after all.

As she was mulling these things over in her head she reached the corner where she had hidden in order to Switch the night before. The big blue van was still there, and she considered using another animal form for her first investigation but, looking around, decided against it. She had nothing to hide after all. She was just a schoolgirl walking along the street. Who would be likely to question her?

Without changing pace she swung round the corner into the street where, she was sure, the Switcher lived. She was slightly disappointed to find that it was completely empty, although if she had been asked what she was expecting to find she wouldn't have been able to say. She strolled slowly along, and was opposite the empty house, just stopping briefly to shift her schoolbag from one shoulder to the other, when a woman came out of her front door and turned into the street towards her. The house she had left was one of the three or four that Tess had targeted as being the most likely. As surreptitiously as she could, she watched the woman approach.

She was about the age of Tess's own mother, but shorter and much, much thinner. She walked with her face turned down towards the pavement, so it wasn't until she was almost level with her that Tess became aware of the most striking thing about the woman. She was deathly pale, paler than anyone Tess had ever seen before. She was so pale that her cheeks were like translucent paper, and Tess had to look closely to be sure that she wasn't wearing some strange kind of make-up or theatrical paint.

Careful as Tess was, the woman became aware of being examined, and looked up quizzically as she passed by. It was clear that she had been crying; her eyes were red-rimmed and puffy, and Tess looked away in embarrassment. She was so disturbed by the strange, pale woman that she almost missed seeing the red-haired boy who stood at the open door, watching after her. As he caught Tess's eye, he gave her the most charming of smiles, so delightful that she smiled back automatically, without thinking. She walked on a few paces before she was struck with an uncanny certainty that it was him. He was the Switcher. He was the right age and lived in one of the likely houses, but it was more than that. It was a feeling of affinity, of some shared experience even though they had never met. Tess stopped and turned round. She didn't know how, but she would find some way to introduce herself.

But when she got back to the door, it was closed. Tess stood there, stunned. The strength of her feeling made no sense to her. She and the boy had never met, so why should he expect her to turn round and come back? Why should the closed door feel so much like a rejection?

And yet it did, and the feeling of disappointment

didn't lessen with time. When she got back home, she was in a foul temper.

'But why?' she said to her mother. 'Why should I always tell you exactly where I'm going to be at any given moment of the day?'

'Because I worry.'

'Why do you worry? You don't trust me, do you?'

'It's not that, Tess. It's . . .'

They both fell silent, each remembering their own, very different sides of Tess's Arctic adventure. As far as Tess had been concerned, it had been imperative for her to go. She realised, however, that for her mother the time she had been away meant no more than a completely unexplained disappearance.

'It upset us, Tess. We were worried.'

'I know you were. But I came back, didn't I? I do my homework every night, I help with the washing-up. It's not as if I'm off carousing every night, is it? You should see some of the other girls in my school, what they get up to!'

Her mother sighed. Tess sighed back, in an exaggerated way, and went upstairs to change. When her father got home, she came down to dinner, ate the biggest meal she had eaten in months and went back upstairs again.

Long before the small hours of the morning, when the phoenix comes into its own, she was fast asleep.

CHAPTER SIX

The following morning, on her way to school in the bus, Tess tried to gather her thoughts. There had been such a whirl of activity in the last two days and nights that she had no idea what was happening and what she should do next. She hated herself for the way she had spoken to her mother, and felt guilty about wanting to leave her parents to be with Kevin and become a phoenix for good. But before she could work out what to do about that, she had to sort out this business about the new Switcher. She had a duty to tell him that his powers would go when he reached his fifteenth birthday, and perhaps to encourage him in some way to learn, as she and Kevin had done, the full extent of his abilities before it was too late.

She wondered how old he was. From the brief glimpse she had got of him, smiling in the doorway, it was hard for her to tell. Younger than she was or older? Not much in it, either way. And how much did he already know? The business with the rats disturbed her. His relationship with them was very different from hers or Kevin's. When they had been among the rats it had been as equals; they learnt from them, and were guided by them on more than one occasion. But this boy, the boy with the strange, mixed-up Rat name, seemed to have a power over them.

Why, though? What did he want? She remembered the message about the stone containers beneath the ground with a strong sense of unease. What was he after? Buried treasure? If so, was it right for him to be using his Switching powers for such purposes: getting the rats to do his dirty work so that he could become rich? Yet if it wasn't right, who was to say? What business was it of hers?

The bus pulled up outside the school and Tess joined the lines of dreary uniformity filing in through the gates. Not much different from the poor old rats, she remarked to herself wryly.

'Still no sign of Algernon, I'm afraid,' her mother said as she began to peel the potatoes that evening. 'I hope he hasn't been caught by a cat or something.'

'So do I,' said Tess. 'I suppose there's nothing we can do about it now.'

'Never mind. We can see about getting another one if he doesn't turn up.'

Tess nodded. 'Anything I can do?'

'You can make a salad if you've finished your homework.'

Tess fetched lettuce and tomatoes from the rack beside the back door and rummaged in the drawer next to the sink for a sharp knife.

'I'm sorry about yesterday evening,' she said.

'About being late and saying you don't trust me. I was a bit tired. And I was upset about Algernon.'

'No.' Her mother looked as though she had a lemon in her mouth, as though what she was saying was difficult for her, but necessary. 'I was thinking about it afterwards, and you were right. You're fourteen now, and what's past is past. I can't go on treating you like a child any more. You do need to have more freedom.'

Tess stayed silent, aware of having won a victory but unsure whether she wanted it or not.

'You have to begin making decisions for yourself,' her mother went on. 'It's only right at your age. You know the dangers of the city, and if you don't understand them by now then you probably never will.'

'It's not as if I want to go off and . . .' Tess lost her thread. Her mother's words were enormously generous, but they also placed a new responsibility on her. It was a big moment.

'I know that, I know that you're not going to get up to mischief. You see, despite . . . despite everything, I do trust you, and so does your father. We were talking about it last night. We think that as long as you keep up with your schoolwork and provided we always know where you are, you ought to be allowed to make more of your own decisions.' She paused for a moment and then added: 'Within reason, of course.'

'You won't worry, then?'

'If I do, it's my problem, isn't it?'

Tess put down her knife, wiped her hands on a tea-towel and flung her arms round her mother's neck.

'Thanks, Mum,' she said. 'You're great, you know that?'

40

Her mother smiled, a little sadly, and Tess saw her as though for the first time: just a woman doing her best in life, as human as everyone else.

The sense of closeness lasted until Tess's father came in a few minutes later. He exchanged the day's news with everyone, as he always did, then settled himself down to read the evening paper until the supper was ready.

'Look at this,' he said, pointing to an item low down on the front page. Tess went across and read over his shoulder. With the first glance at the headline her heart began to sink.

RARE BIRD CAPTURED IN THE PHOENIX PARK
In the early hours of this morning, head zoo-keeper Jeff Maloney, with the help of two assistant zoo-keepers, netted a rare bird which was discovered in a tree at the edge of the Phoenix Park. The bird had been sighted the previous night, but was gone by the time Mr Maloney arrived on the scene. Last night, however, he was well prepared and arrived in good time to find the bird roosting on an outer branch of the tree. The bird offered no resistance to being captured and was clearly quite at ease when handled. This suggests that it has escaped from some other collection, perhaps a private one, but so far no one has reported it missing.

The bird is said to be about two and a half feet in length with small wings and long tail feathers. It is golden in colour and, unlike some species of domestic and wild fowl which are also described as golden, it has no black markings whatsoever. At the time of writing, the experts at the zoo have failed to identify the bird.

By the time Tess had finished reading the report, she was leaning against the back of her father's chair, willing her shaking legs to bear her weight. How could this have happened? Why on earth hadn't he flown away? And the worst thought of all was: would it have happened if I hadn't been fast asleep at the time?

'There was some sort of activity going on outside here last night,' said Tess's mother, who was also reading the report. 'I thought it was some people come back from a party, getting excited about something and banging car doors. Do you think it was something to do with the bird?'

'It's possible,' said her father.

Tess's legs weren't responding as required, and she had slumped into an armchair in the corner. Now she dropped her head into her hands in despair. What would they do with him? How could she find him, let alone get around to setting him free?

Her mother checked the potatoes and drained them, then began to set out the meal. 'Are you all right, Tess?' she asked.

Tess stood up. There was no way she could just sit there and keep her emotions hidden, pretending that nothing had happened. 'I won't be having any dinner, if you don't mind. I have to go and look for someone.'

'What? Look for who? And your dinner's on the table – why don't you just have a bite before you go?'

'No, thanks.' Tess was already on her way out of the kitchen and collecting her coat in the hall.

Her mother followed. 'But Tess . . .'

Tess's emotions got the upper hand. 'But Tess, but Tess,' she said angrily. 'It's fine in theory, isn't it, saying that you trust me. In practice it's different, isn't it?'

There was a heavy silence between them, during which Tess could hear her father push back his chair and cross the room towards them. Then her mother sighed and turned away. 'OK, Tess,' she said. 'But be back before ten o'clock, all right?'

Tess nodded and shot out of the door, pulling on her coat as she went. As the door closed her father said, 'What was all that about?'

Her mother shrugged. 'She's a teenager,' she said. 'What do you expect?'

Outside the door, Tess buttoned her coat against a damp westerly wind. She had let down her hair when she got home, and now it began to fly around, getting in her eyes and obscuring her vision. She felt in her pocket. There was loose change in there, and her door key, but no hair band. She stuffed her hair down the back of her collar and looked around.

She had come out with no clear idea of what she was going to do. Her first thought was to go to Phibsboro to try and find the Switcher and enlist his help, but she realised now that she had no idea of what she would be asking him to do. Until she knew where the phoenix was, there could be no plan made for releasing him.

She walked along the street until she felt safe from watching eyes, then she crossed over into the shade of the trees, where she was hidden from the street lights. It was a short walk across the park to the zoo, but in human form she would have no chance of getting inside and looking around. She cut across an open space, checking to be sure that there were no people around, and made for the cover of a small stand of trees, where she Switched into an owl. Within a minute she was approaching the zoo, but it became apparent that her choice of bird was not of the best. The buildings were ablaze with light, which blinded her so badly that she became disorientated and had to make an emergency landing in a nearby tree. She considered trying a bat, even though she knew it was their time of year for hibernation, but when she thought about it further she realised that would not serve her purpose either. The bat's sonic system would tell her a certain amount and avoid the confusion of light, but she would have no way of seeing inside the buildings since the sound would bounce back from the glass windows and tell her nothing of what lay behind them.

She needed sight. What creature could find its way through the darkness but not be dazzled by bright light? A cat would do it, but then a cat might attract too much attention and be too slow to escape. The last thing she wanted was to be collared herself.

The answer came to her in an instant. When they had lived in a wooded area of the countryside, she had made the acquaintance of a pine marten, who had often come to visit even on days when she didn't Switch and go to find him. The pine marten had become a sort of family pet, and they left food out for him on the porch outside the back door. The house lights had never bothered him, and he seemed to be able to see perfectly well when he came to the kitchen door and poked his nose in.

As she Switched, Tess realised that the pine marten had other advantages, too. It was as fast as greased lightning if threatened, and it could climb; not only up and down trees, but on surfaces that were almost smooth. She shinned down the tree in which she had made such a clumsy landing, and raced across the grass towards the zoo. As she ran, she remembered how the long, sinewy body felt from inside; its wiry strength and its quickness and its cunning. The pine marten was afraid of very little in life. There were few dangers which it could not avoid with its remarkable speed and agility.

A guard stood at the entrance gate of the zoo. As Tess watched, a taxi pulled up and let out a group of men and women in smart clothes. The guard checked their identification, then made a call on a portable phone before letting them through and pointing out their destination with a series of gestures. While his attention was taken up with that, Tess slipped beneath a turnstile and into the grounds.

There was plenty of cover for a pine marten. The areas between the roads were covered in low shrubs which smelt enticingly of domestic fowl: ducks and peacocks and guinea-hens. With an effort, Tess brought her mind back to the business in hand. The new arrivals were making their way towards the hexagonal aviary, and Tess followed at a distance, on silent paws. Outside the aviary door a second guard was standing, and he, too, talked into a mobile phone before opening the door with a key and locking it again behind them.

Tess lay low and watched carefully. All around the outside of the building were wire pens which connected to the cages inside, so that on fine days the birds could be allowed out into the open. They were all vacant now; the sharp eyes of the pine marten could have picked out a roosting bird no matter how well camouflaged it was. If the phoenix was in there, and the flow of activity suggested that it probably was, she would have to find some way of getting close enough to the door to see inside. That was going to be tricky, with the guard standing there. A pine marten is as big as a cat, and there was no cover close to the door; no way to stay hidden.

Tess used both her minds together and eventually

45

came up with a solution. The outside pens were enclosed by strong wire netting, and if she could sneak around and scale the furthest one, round the other side, she would be able to cross the tops of them until she got to the front again, where she would be in a perfect position to see into the door the next time it opened.

Taking a long way round, she approached the pens. With a jump and a scramble she was up, and slinking silently along the top of the cages to the door. There she settled herself to wait.

It seemed like hours before the door eventually opened again and a group of people came out; many more than Tess had seen go in. A man at the back was talking loudly, and Tess knew that he was feeling very proud of himself even though she couldn't understand, with the pine marten's brain, what he was saying. She edged forward, stretching down to try and see through the door. No one looked up; all were too busy talking in excited voices. Tess stretched still further, her body becoming longer and longer as her front paws walked down the edge of the net and her back paws held tight, keeping her anchored. Still she couldn't see around the angle of the door, and in another minute the last of the people would be out and the door would close again. In a moment of desperate courage, Tess made a flying leap and landed on the ground between two of the departing guests, who sprang back in shock. She was only on the ground for a split second, but that split second was all she needed to get a glimpse inside the door. Then she was gone, racing away through the under-growth and leaping up the netted wire which ran between the zoo and the main road through the park.

The various experts on birds and wildlife who had

been inspecting the strange new find were puzzled by the sight of the pine marten, but not as puzzled as Jeff Maloney was. Before he left for home that evening, he checked the enclosure where the pine martens lived, and was even more surprised to find that neither of its occupants was missing.

CHAPTER SEVEN

The sound of the morning paper being pulled through the letter box woke Tess. It was Saturday, and there was no reason for her to get up for another hour or two, but she jumped out of bed and pulled on her dressing-gown.

Her father was making coffee when she got into the kitchen. The paper was folded beside his place at the head of the table, but Tess got to it first. On the front page, beneath the main item on the failure of peace talks in the North, was a feature about the golden bird.

'Your mother was worried about you last night,' her father said.

'Why? I was back before ten o'clock, wasn't I?'

'And why do you have to be so mysterious about where you were?'

Tess felt her irritation rising. She wanted to read

the piece in the paper without a cross-examination. 'I was visiting a friend.'

'What friend? Since when have you had friends that you go to visit? You never bring them here.'

'I can't, not this one, anyway. He's not allowed out.'

'Oh? Why's that?'

'Maybe they're afraid he'll disappear.'

Her father began to say something more, but thought better of it. Tess returned to the paper.

US COLLECTOR TO BUY
PHOENIX PARK PHOENIX

Officials of the Dublin Zoo have today confirmed that the mysterious bird captured two nights ago in the Phoenix Park is to be sold to a private collector based in Missouri, USA. The figure involved has not been disclosed, but it is said to be 'fabulous'. Zoo officials say that it will allow for a complete refurbishment of certain areas of the zoo compound, as well as providing funds for the purchase and housing of a number of new animals: endangered species in particular.

The government has sanctioned the decision, on the condition that the 'phoenix' be kept for one week at the Dublin Zoo, and made available for public viewing. To this end, a special display unit is under construction, and the zoo will be open from 10 a.m. to 6 p.m. from Monday 16th to Sunday 2nd February.

The Head Keeper at the zoo, Mr Jeff Maloney, confirmed that there had been initial difficulties in finding out the diet of the mysterious bird. While this had caused serious concern, it has now been resolved. The phoenix has revealed a partiality for fresh apricots, cashew nuts and spring water, and is now feeding regularly. Its condition is described as 'excellent'.

Tess handed the paper over to her father and waited while he read the article. As soon as he had finished, she said, 'Can I go?'

'Of course. I'll go with you, if you like.'

Tess spent the morning in town with her parents, struggling against a growing frustration and impatience. She urgently wanted to get to Phibsboro and find a way of looking up the boy, but she couldn't push her luck with her parents. Saturday-morning shopping was a ritual, and so was Saturday lunch in town.

It was after two when they got home. Tess ran upstairs and changed into a new pair of jeans that her mother had bought for her, then came back down.

'What's time's dinner?' she asked, pocketing a banana and an apple.

'The usual time, I suppose,' said her mother. 'Why? Where are you going?'

'To visit a friend in Phibsboro. I won't be late.'

Before her mother could reply, Tess grabbed her jacket and raced out into the street. She ran across the corner of the park to the Navan Road and began to walk quickly, checking over her shoulder from time to time for the bus. By the time one came and stopped for her, she had walked half-way to Phibsboro, but she felt so anxious about the captured phoenix that every minute mattered. It was an expensive two stops, but worth it to her.

A few young children were playing soccer in the street where the Switcher lived. They looked Tess over suspiciously before resuming their game. The door of the red-headed boy's house was closed. There was no car parked in front of it and no sound of a

50

television or radio coming from within. Tess hesitated before knocking, aware of the eyes of the soccer players returning to her, aware that despite spending most of the morning trying to work out what she would say when that door opened, she still hadn't come to any firm decisions.

Her stomach was in knots. It would be so much easier just to turn and walk away. But without help, how was she going to go about releasing the phoenix? She hadn't even come up with a plan yet.

Tess knocked and waited. If there was no one there it would at least solve the immediate problem. She was just raising her hand to knock again when she heard the latch turn. The door opened a crack and the face of the pale woman peered out.

'Yes?'

Tess's mouth moved, groping for words that didn't come.

'Can I help you?'

'I was looking for ... have you got a son? Red hair?'

The woman opened the door another inch but only, it seemed, to scrutinise Tess in an extremely suspicious manner.

'Who are you?' she said.

'I . . I'm a friend. I wanted to ask him for some help.' She would get herself into deep water if she wasn't careful.

'Martin hasn't got any friends. What sort of help are you looking for?'

Tess's mind went blank. The thin woman opened the door and folded her arms.

'It's a sort of project,' said Tess, lamely. 'To do with birds.'

For a long moment Martin's mother stared hard

at Tess, but gradually her gaze began to soften and be replaced with something slightly less hostile.

'Well,' she said at last, 'you can only try. He's in his room, sleeping, probably. Why don't you go on up and see if you can get him out of bed?'

Tess nodded and stepped inside.

'First door on the left at the top of the stairs. Let me know if you need anything, won't you? Like a straitjacket or a tranquilliser gun.'

Tess turned to share the joke with the woman, but she was merely looking up the stairs, her white face drawn with anxiety. With mounting apprehension, Tess started up.

The house was unusually dark. The window at the top of the stairs which ought to have lit the landing had been replaced by dimpled yellow glass; the type that is sometimes found in bathrooms. There was something eerie about the silence up there which made it difficult for Tess to muster the courage to knock on the bedroom door. Martin, he was called. She remembered his charming smile. Surely there was nothing to fear?

She knocked and waited. Nothing happened. She knocked again, and then a third time.

'Martin?' she called. 'Hello?'

Nothing. She knocked again, then leant against the wall, wondering what to do next. There was no sound from below, and she wondered what the boy's mother was doing down there. She had the impression that the rest of the house must somehow be as dark as this landing, and it gave her the creeps. She longed to turn back, to just slip quietly down the stairs and out of the door without telling anyone, but she knew that if she did that she would never have the courage to come back again. If she was going to make contact with Martin, it was now or never. Steeling herself, she reached out and quietly turned the door handle.

It wasn't locked. The door opened stiffly, rubbing against the dark grey carpet within. The curtains were drawn and only a suggestion of daylight made its way through them. In the opposite corner was a bed, and as Tess's eyes grew accustomed to the gloom she could just make out the shape of the boy, lying on his back.

'Hello?' she said, but quietly. The atmosphere was so heavy that she dared not speak any louder. There was no response, so she crossed the room, taking care not to disturb any of the clutter which covered most of the floor.

Martin showed no sign of hearing her approach. His face, when she drew near, was not as pale as his mother's, but there was a darkness around his eyes as though he were in the habit of not getting enough sleep. Tess wondered whether she was making a mistake in coming to wake him. Perhaps there were family troubles? Perhaps he was an insomniac and this was the only sleep he had managed to get in days?

'Martin?' she said, gently. Still the boy's eyes didn't open, and Tess realised with a shock that she could see no sign of movement from his chest to signify that he was breathing. What if he was dead and his mother didn't know? What if she did know?

Suddenly Tess had had enough of the darkness and enough of feeling afraid. With a new sense of purpose she strode across the room, knocking her knee against a stack of magazines as she did so, then pulled back the curtains. The rings squealed on the rail as though protesting against the flood of early-evening light.

'Martin!' said Tess, with as much firmness in her voice as she could manage.

The boy cried out softly as though he had been robbed of something precious, then opened his eyes.

'What is it?' he said. 'Who's there?'

'It's me. My name's Tess. I saw you on the street a few days ago, remember?'

Martin looked at her blearily for a moment, then sat up.

'Have you come to help?' he said.

'Help with what?'

Martin looked away for a moment, then turned back. Once again his face wore the sweet smile that had stayed in her mind's eye for so long.

'Do you need help with something?' she said.

He laughed and shook his head, and Tess had a strange sense of having missed some kind of opportunity.

'Are you sure?' she said.

'I'm sure.'

'Well, I do.'

'Oh?'

She stopped, remembering the difficulty that Kevin had encountered when he tried to convince her that he knew she was a Switcher. It was something that had been private for her all her life, and it was a subject not easy to approach. She had been defensive and dismissive. She had no reason to believe that Martin wouldn't feel the same way.

'It's a friend of mine,' she said at last. 'Sort of a friend, anyway. He's been taken prisoner.'

'By who?' Martin's face seemed to be open and full of concern, but Tess was aware of some darkness which flitted behind his eyes.

'By the zoo,' she said.

54

'The zoo?' said Martin, his voice full of incredulity. Tess had hoped that it might have been enough of a hint; that if he was a Switcher he would empathise with her having animal friends and open himself to her. But instead he went on, 'Are you serious? Are you the full shilling?'

Tess swore to herself in Rat. There was no easy way into this. 'Look,' she said, 'let's not beat about the bush, eh? I know who you are, I know what you can do. You don't have to pretend with me.'

The boy ran a hand through his thick red hair and looked at Tess with a bemused expression. 'What, exactly, do you know?' he asked. Again his face seemed open and friendly, but again Tess was aware of a shadow passing behind his eyes, as though there were someone else in there apart from the charming boy, looking out through his eyes.

Tess took the bull by the horns. 'I know that you're a Switcher. I know that because I'm one, too.'

'A Switcher?' Martin's face wore a puzzled frown. 'What's a Switcher?'

'You know very well, because you are one.'

'I know what I am, all right,' said Martin, and there was an edge to his voice as he said it which went along with the sinister shadow in his eyes. 'What I don't know, though, is what it has to do with you.'

'I've already told you. I need your help to rescue my friend. I don't know how I'm going to do it on my own.'

Martin looked thoughtfully at his feet for a moment, then said, 'Tell me about your friend.'

CHAPTER EIGHT

Tess wasn't sure where to start. She realised she was still standing up beside the bed, and took the opportunity to get her thoughts together while she looked for a chair. There was one beside the table, but she had to move a pile of books off it. She noticed as she did so that they were all horror stories, classics as well as modern writers.

'How old are you?' she asked, as she brought the chair over to the bed and sat down in it.

Martin resettled himself as well, propping himself up on pillows and pulling the covers up around his waist.

'Fifteen,' he said.

The wind was knocked out of Tess's sails, and for a moment she wondered if she was making a terrible mistake.

'You can't be!' she said.

'Well I am, almost. Why shouldn't I be?'

Tess breathed a sigh of relief. 'Because if you were, if you'd had your fifteenth birthday, you wouldn't be able to do it any more.'

'Do what?'

'You know very well, what. Change your form, become something else.'

The look in Martin's eye was, for a moment, openly hostile. In an instant, though, he had recovered his poise, and the charming expression of puzzled interest returned.

'Go on,' he said.

'Well, you need to know that, because whatever you are on your fifteenth birthday is what you'll stay. You need to have time to think about it.'

Martin shook his head. 'Not me,' he said. 'I already know what I'm going to be. I mightn't even wait until my fifteenth birthday.'

It was the acceptance that Tess had been waiting for, but she was careful not to show her satisfaction.

'I feel like that, too,' she said. 'But I can't do anything about it until I've got my friend out of the zoo.'

'Ah, yes. Your friend. You were going to tell me about your friend.'

Tess relaxed and began to tell the story of her meeting with Kevin and the adventure which had brought them to the Arctic Circle to battle against the krools. It was wonderful to be able to relive her experiences once more, with someone who understood and seemed to appreciate them. She told him everything, right up to Kevin's return and his capture by the zoo authorities, and then she fell silent. Martin was silent, too, and Tess had the impression that he wasn't sure whether to believe her or not. In any event, it was clear that he wasn't going to admit that he was impressed. Outside a few birds were beginning their evening song, and on the street below the game of soccer was still going on. As the two Switchers sat there, each engrossed in his or her own thoughts, Martin's mother appeared in the doorway, looking anxious and eager to please.

'A cup of tea?' she said.

Martin nodded without a word, and his mother smiled in acknowledgement. 'Everything all right?'

Again the boy nodded. His mother departed, as though she had been dismissed. Tess was shocked. She turned to Martin, meaning to remark on the nature of his behaviour, but he was smiling so sweetly that she was disarmed.

'How did you find out about me?' he asked.

Tess told him about Algernon and her journey through the city in response to his call.

'What do you want with those stone boxes, anyway?' she asked.

Martin rubbed his chin and looked heavenward, musing. Then he said, 'Let's just say that I have a certain interest in archaeology, shall we?'

'But why?'

'Why not? There are probably hundreds of ancient structures beneath the city that have never been excavated. I'd like to know where some of them are, that's all.'

Tess wasn't entirely happy with the explanation, but she didn't feel she could push it any further. Besides, there were more important matters to be sorted out.

'Well, what about it?' she said.

'What about what?'

'About the phoenix. Will you help me to get him out?'

'How do you propose to do it?'

'I'm not sure, yet. Maybe we could come up with a plan together? I'm sure we could get some help from the rats if we needed to.'

'Hmm.' Martin hitched himself up in the bed and rearranged his pillows. 'The rats are fairly busy at the moment. Besides, I'm bored with all that squirrel and bunny stuff. I've grown out of it, you know?'

'Who said anything about squirrels and bunnies?' said Tess. 'I was a pine marten yesterday and it was brilliant! In any case, I can't see how squirrels and bunnies are going to help get Kevin out.'

'No. You know what I mean, though. It's all a bit tame, isn't it?' Martin was looking into space as he spoke, as though seeing something in his mind's eye that Tess had no conception of. She was about to ask him what he meant when his mother appeared again at the door with a tray of tea things. She had moved so softly that Tess hadn't heard her approach, and she hoped that she hadn't overheard anything she shouldn't.

Martin made no move to help his mother with the tray, so Tess got up and cleared a space on the table. She was shocked again by the drained, bloodless look on the woman's face and by the way her hands and arms trembled as though the effort of carrying the tray upstairs had been too much for her.

'Everybody happy?' she said.

'Yes, thanks,' said Tess.

'You can pour, I suppose?'

'Of course I can,' said Tess.

Martin's mother turned to leave, but before she did so, Tess thought she caught an expression of gratitude on her face.

'Why is she so pale?' she asked Martin, after a safe length of time had passed.

Martin shrugged, and a queer little smirk crossed his mouth. 'The doctor says she's anaemic. He doesn't know why.'

'Why don't you help her? You could have made that tea yourself, you know.'

Again Martin shrugged. 'Mothers,' he said. 'You know what they're like. They don't want you to grow up because then they have to let you go.'

Tess felt an intense irritation towards the slovenly boy, lying in bed waiting to be spoon-fed. She wanted to tell him to pour his own tea or go without it, but her nerve failed her. If she got on the wrong side of him he might refuse to help her, and she didn't believe that she could liberate Kevin on her own. Suppressing her anger, she filled two cups and handed one across. Martin took it without thanking her.

'Do you want to watch a video?' he asked. 'My mother will go and get one if you do.'

Tess noticed for the first time that there was a TV and video recorder in the corner of the room beside the window, placed so that Martin could watch from the bed.

'No, thanks,' she said, struggling now with her still-rising anger. 'And if I did want to watch one I'd get it myself.'

Infuriatingly, Martin giggled. Tess sipped her tea and looked at her feet. However weak he was, she needed him. She would have to get help from him even if she had to beg for it.

'Will you help me?' she asked.

'I might.' He thought for a moment, then seemed

to come to a decision. 'I'll tell you what. I'll consider helping you to get your friend out on one condition.'

'What's that?'

'Well. You've told me about your adventures, and what you've learnt to do with your powers. I'd like you to know what I've learnt as well. How does that sound?'

'Sounds great.'

'Good. Only I'd prefer to show you than tell you. Does that make any sense?'

'I suppose it does.'

'Right. Come here tonight, then, and we can do the rounds together, OK?'

'This evening?'

'Tonight would be better. When dear mother is asleep. Say, one o'clock?'

Tess groaned inwardly. Another sleepless night. Another night of worry about leaving the house and getting back in time. But it had to be worth it.

'It might be a bit later,' she said, 'but I'll be there.'

CHAPTER NINE

That night, soon after midnight, two figures walked quietly down a street in Phibsboro. A heavy frost was beginning to spangle the grass in the gardens they passed, and their breath curled billows of steam around them as they walked.

'Warm enough?' said Martin, as they turned the corner of the street where he lived.

'Just about,' said Tess, pulling her scarf up over her mouth and nose. 'You must be freezing, though.'

'I am,' he said, 'but I won't be for long.'

They crossed the street and walked past an off-licence with padlocked aluminium shutters over all the windows, then turned on to the main road which ran from the outskirts of Dublin in towards the city centre.

'Where are we going?' asked Tess.

'Nowhere in particular. Just walking.'

'Why?'

'You'll see.'

Tess stuffed her hands deeper into her pockets, feeling irritated by Martin's secretiveness. What could be so special, after all? She followed rather sullenly as Martin crossed one small intersection in the road, then another. A few cars passed, every second one a taxi, bringing people home from the pubs.

Ahead of them, at the next intersection, was a red brick building which sold carpets and upholstery fabric. Outside, a group of young men were gathered, smoking and swigging from beer bottles, tussling with each other and laughing. Tess slowed down, uneasy about passing them by.

'Shouldn't we cross over?' she said, coming to a halt on the footpath.

Martin turned to her with a smile, and as he did so it seemed to Tess that the darkness she had glimpsed behind his eyes earlier in the day had come right up to the front and was leering out at her in mockery.

'Why?' he said.

Tess faltered, all her courage leaving her. She had a strong desire to Switch, to become a rat and scuttle down the nearest drain, or a creature with wings, to fly her out of there. The boys on the corner had noticed them now and they became quiet, all their attention turned towards the two strangers. Tess pulled her coat tighter around her, aware as she did so that it had been bought in one of the swankiest shops in town. It told everything about her and her family. Even though she had no money on her, she was an obvious target for anyone with mugging on their mind.

'Martin,' she said, her voice pleading for reason.

From the corner of her eye she saw the group of lads gather together and begin to advance.

Martin smiled, or leered, at her again. 'Just watch,' he said. He began to walk forwards. It was too late now for Tess to break off on her own and cross the road. It was even too late to run. In a few quick strides she drew level with Martin, just as the first of the young men stepped into their path.

In that instant, Martin Switched. Tess saw and felt the strange fuzziness in the air around him as he lost substance and regained it again. She shivered; her mind was caught up in the moment of vacancy, then began casting around for the new form that Martin had taken. He had turned slightly away from her as he Switched, and it seemed as she looked at him that nothing had changed. He was still a boy in a light anorak, standing quietly in the edge of a street-lamp's glow. But as she watched, she became aware that there had, indeed, been a change. Even before she noticed the gang of boys backing off, Tess could feel some sort of power radiating from Martin. It attracted and repelled her at the same time, so that she didn't know whether to move away from him or towards him. As she stood still, trying to understand what was happening, the lads retreated towards the brighter light beneath the lamp-post and stood there uncertainly, huddled together.

Then Martin turned to face her. Tess's heart lurched. In a sense the boy in front of her was still Martin, but at the same time he wasn't. His face was deathly pale apart from his lips, which were strangely red and protruding, as though the teeth inside the mouth were too big to fit properly. The eyes which gazed out at her were dull and lifeless, yet they latched on to something within her, drawing her in, making it impossible for her to move away. As she gazed in a grim mixture of fear and attraction she knew what had happened, she knew what he was, but she just couldn't put a name on it. Until he smiled.

The only experience Tess could remember which had anything of the horror of this one was the time the first krool had suddenly reared up before her in the Arctic. That time she had reacted without thought; this time there was no reaction apart from complete paralysis. For when Martin, or the thing that had been Martin a few minutes ago, smiled, it revealed a pair of razor-sharp fangs, so long that they reached down over the bottom teeth and were hidden by the bulging lower lip.

'Well?' he said. His voice was smooth and seductive. Tess looked over at the lamp-post, and as she did so two of the boys there made a sudden dart across the road. She turned back to the vampire, still leering at her, showing his fangs. As a boy he had been a moderate sort of height, but now he seemed to tower above her, sneering down.

Tess looked at her feet. There was a scuffle as the other boys raced across the road to join their friends and she felt suddenly alone. A few minutes ago those lads had been her enemies, but now that she was faced with this monstrous creature they seemed to be allies and she felt abandoned by them and desperately alone.

'Are you going to back out on me?' said Martin.

Tess looked up, trying to avoid the lure of those vacuous eyes but failing. 'What do you mean, back out?'

'You promised to try my way, remember?'

Tess shuddered with revulsion. 'I . . .'

'You what?' The voice was like sleep, sucking at her mind, dragging her under. She struggled.

'I didn't know,' she shouted. 'You didn't tell me!'

The vampire's smile broadened. 'You didn't ask,' said the creamy voice.

Tess felt sick. What stood in front of her wasn't Martin. It was something that was dead and yet lived on, undead. She understood now why he had said that he wouldn't be cold for long. Vampires didn't feel the cold. They didn't feel anything at all, in any way. Tess knew beyond doubt as she looked into those dark eyes that there was no appeal under the sun that would release her from his power. She did not exist for him as an equal being at all. To him she was nothing more than an object, a victim, the source of his next meal.

Behind her she heard the sound of a car drawing up close to the kerb. Martin closed his lips over his teeth and glanced up over her shoulder to see who was behind her. Tess closed her eyes, released for a moment from that dreadful gaze, and fear welled up within her. She began to turn towards the car, ready to scream out for help, but even as she did so the car started to draw away. The garda in the passenger seat nodded towards Martin as his partner drove off. Tess called out, but it was too late. Beside her, Martin was exuding charm again, and before she could tear herself away he slipped a strong arm around her and began to walk up the quiet street which led away from the main road, into the darkness.

Tess tried to struggle but it was useless. The vampire was strong beyond imagining, and already his power was beginning to take over her mind again, drawing her in to the vacuum of his heart. At a corner beneath a tall sycamore tree, he stopped, and Tess leant against the wall, looking down at the ground. Leaves and sweet wrappers and crisp bags had gathered there during the last windy day. Martin leaned towards her. His voice was a harsh whisper in her ear.

'It's up to you. You can join me if you want to, but if you don't . . .'

He smiled again, that sinister smile that was as cold and distant as the moon. Tess knew what he meant. He was in front of her now, blocking any escape she might attempt. His breath was cold on her face and had a faint metallic scent.

Her mind felt slow and cumbersome, numbed by her fear. She could think of no creature on earth that would be a sure protection against the power that confronted her now; certainly there was none that could kill him. How can you kill what is already dead?

Slowly, inch by inch, his face was coming closer to hers, his head bowing, his teeth approaching her neck. The knowledge, when it came to her, seemed always to have been there, perfect in its logic. There was only one protection against a being like this, and that was to become like him. She resisted, waiting for the last moment, desperately searching her mind for an alternative.

His breath, colder than the frosty air surrounding them, touched her neck, freezing the area where he planned to bite. She was in an impossible position; whichever course she took seemed like a submission. She tried to dodge out to the side, but he was quicker. She thumped and pushed at his shoulders and knees, but he was like a statue: cold and immovable. His teeth met her neck; she felt the pressure of their points against her skin, and as they broke through she began to drift down, down, away from consciousness, into a dark oblivion.

'No!

At the moment that she shouted, Tess Switched. Martin drew back and regarded her, his cynical smile tinged now with an element of respect and comradeship. Tess returned it, feeling the new shape of her mouth as it accommodated those deadly teeth. She ran her tongue over them, careful of their sharpness, and lifted a hand to her face. The external change was small. She still fitted into her clothes; if she met someone she knew they would probably recognise her. But the internal change was enormous. Without ever testing it, she knew that she was possessed of fantastic strength and that no living person could stand up to her. And her mental strength was no less: a storehouse of power, just waiting to be used. The only problem was a deep and urgent hunger which could only be satisfied by one thing.

Without a word, Martin and Tess linked arms with each other. From a distance they were like two young lovers strolling down the street, as innocent as spring.

CHAPTER TEN

The city belonged to Tess and Martin. By night, there is nothing under the sky that vampires fear, for nothing can harm them. It is only by day, when they sleep away the hours of daylight, that fear impinges upon their dreams and makes their rest uneasy.

The two Switchers crossed the road and followed the route the gang of boys had taken, towards the centre of the city. At the next junction they veered to the left, heading for the docks and the darkness. They moved swiftly and silently, but if anyone noticed their strong strides and solemn deportment, they didn't stop to question them.

Tess gloried in the dark power she found within herself. She had experienced many kinds of strength in the past, in the different animal forms she had assumed, but she had never imagined that a human shape could make her feel like this. It was wonderful to be able to walk the city streets at night in full view of any watching eyes and know that she was invulnerable. She could do anything, go anywhere she liked; no one could stop her, no one could harm her in any way.

She turned towards her companion and the two of them exchanged grim smiles of complicity. But even as they did so, Tess knew that she wouldn't care if she never saw him again. Let them hunt together tonight; let her learn from him whatever she had to know. After that she was on her own, gloriously alone, for ever.

Literally for ever. For all eternity. Because vampires live for ever, spreading their condition like a disease to everyone they feed upon. Unless they are unlucky, that is. Unless someone discovers their existence and tracks them down to their hiding place and drives a stake through their heart. But who, these days, believes in vampires?

Tess laughed to herself, quietly, and discovered the new sound of her voice. She liked it; it was dark and husky, as different from her human voice as Martin's was from his. She knew that it would be as hypnotic to a potential victim as a mongoose's dance is to a snake. All she needed now was an opportunity to try it out.

Although it was the early hours of the morning, the streets were not empty. Taxis serviced the night-life of the city, twisting through the quiet streets. Occasionally a police car cruised past; occasionally a speeding biker, revving hard. Drifters idled their way home from pubs and night-clubs, and homeless people beat the streets to keep themselves warm. Every time they came within a few metres of another human being, Tess felt her hunger gnaw at her, as though she had come in from a long day at school and smelt dinner roasting in the oven. But her companion kept well away from anyone else on the street, and she decided to stay close. The two of them let everything pass them by, like lions walking peacefully through a herd of small game, their attention fixed on better things.

'Why the docks?' said Tess, as they first came in sight of the river.

'Good hunting ground,' said Martin.

'But we've passed plenty of possibilities,' said Tess. 'What's so special about the docks?'

'Dark, for one thing,' said Martin. 'And for another thing, who wants to drink the blood of boozers and dossers? It's weak and impure. Gives me a headache.'

Tess looked at him carefully, but he didn't appear to be joking. He pulled up his coat collar as he stepped on to the bridge and, aware of the bright street lights all the way across, Tess followed suit.

On the other side of the river they turned right. A few cars were parked beside the road, and in one of them two men were sitting. Tess glanced through the window as she passed by. One of the men was reading a newspaper, the other was pulling absently at the crease in his trousers.

'No good?' she said to Martin as they walked on.

'Cops,' he said. 'Plain clothes. Not bad, if you like cholesterol.'

Tess peered into his shaded eyes and he grinned at her. This time he was joking.

'My tastes aren't that refined,' he said. 'Not yet, anyway. Too much light, though. Be patient.'

They walked on until they came to the first of the ships moored up against the river wall, then crossed over the road and turned up a dark side-street.

'Now we're in good hunting grounds,' said Martin.

He slowed the pace a bit and became more watchful, looking casually but carefully into parked cars and checking out the yards that opened off the street. On the corner, a man and a woman were sitting in a high-bodied van. They looked anxiously at the two Switchers as they passed. Martin took no notice of them.

'Dealers,' he said. 'Small fry, though. They use drugs themselves, just deal to feed their habit. If you could get the guy who supplies them, now, you'd be on to a good thing.'

'Why?'

'Because they're usually clean, those fellows. Too careful to get mixed up in the stuff themselves.' He chuckled to himself in a manner that Tess might have found sinister on another occasion, then went on, 'I've had a good guzzle or two on that kind. Very clean, they tend to be. Very well fed.'

'Why don't we wait here, then?' said Tess. 'Someone's going to come and supply those two in the van, aren't they?'

'I doubt it. That's what the cops are thinking, too. That's why they're there. But the big fish are too smart to get copped that easily. They're somewhere else, you can be sure, laughing their heads off at this lot.'

Tess shrugged and kept pace with Martin as he strode through the streets, always seeking out the darkest ones. As they turned yet another corner, they caught a glimpse of a woman in high heels running across the junction at the other end. Tess's hopes rose. She knew that the two of them could have been on her in a few powerful strides, like greyhounds on a hare, but once again Martin shook his head.

Tess was beginning to lose patience. 'Why not?' she said. 'What on earth was wrong with that one?'

'Nothing, as far as I know,' said Martin. 'But why run when you don't have to? It's undignified.'

'What do I care about dignity?' said Tess. 'I'm hungry.'

Martin stopped abruptly and swung around to face her. 'Hungry?' he said. 'What do you know of the hunger of a vampire, eh? I mean the real hunger, not your pathetic peckishness?'

Tess felt her lips draw away from her teeth in an automatic, defensive sneer.

'You'd better not be hungry,' Martin went on. 'Not really hungry, I mean. We can live for a long, long time on these streets without raising anyone's suspicions, but not if we let our appetites run away with us.'

'I don't know what you're talking about,' said Tess.

'I'm talking about the difference between keeping the wolf from the door and having a real feed. The fact is, you can't be that hungry, any more than I can, because you've had your breakfast and your dinner and your tea at home, haven't you?'

Tess was about to tell him that she hadn't, in fact; what she had eaten that day was breakfast, lunch and dinner, but she decided against it. 'More or less,' she said.

'Right,' Martin went on. 'But if you hadn't, and if you didn't have them yesterday, either, then you'd be really dangerous.'

'To who?'

'To us. Because when you pulled someone in and started feeding, you wouldn't be able to stop.'

'So what?'

'So they'd find a dead body, drained of blood, wouldn't they? With two tiny incisions on the neck.'

'But no one believes in vampires these days.'

'No. But they soon would if it happened often enough, wouldn't they?'

Tess shrugged. 'Who cares, anyway?'

'I do,' said Martin, with cold determination. 'I plan to live in this city for a very long time. A very, very long time. And I don't plan on being discovered. That means we have to go carefully, drink little and often, so as not to make people suspicious.'

Tess looked up and down the street, sighing with incredulity. 'You're mad, do you know that?' she said. 'You're going to feed off a different person every night and you think you can get away with it? You think your victims are going to shake your hand and say, "You're welcome, come again?" Don't be ridiculous! All right, the police won't believe the first person who complains, but they'll believe the tenth and the eleventh and the twenty-first!'

The creamy quality slipped back into Martin's voice. 'You haven't read the literature, have you?'

'What literature?'

'All there is. On vampires. Our victims forget, didn't you know that? They pass out as we feed and go to sleep. When they wake up they feel a bit weak and fuzzy-headed, but they have no memory of us at all. And who's going to notice a couple of pinpricks on their throat? Specially if we're careful.'

Tess looked Martin straight in the eye, still wishing she could win the point but knowing she was beaten. At last she smiled mischievously, and nodded.

'Understood,' she said.

They resumed their patrol, silent and agile as cats on the frosty street. They turned again, following the darkness wherever they could and then, as they passed the open doors of an abandoned coal-merchant's, Martin stopped and sniffed the air. Tess joined him and immediately caught the same scent. There were two people nearby. Very nearby.

Stealthily, the two vampires slipped into the yard. In the nearest corner, hidden from the street by the open corrugated iron door, a car was parked. Quite a new car, clean and without a scratch. Martin crouched low and crept up to the driver's door, Tess on his heels. Under the cover of almost perfect darkness, they peered into the car, their vampire eyes penetrating the dim interior. Tess had expected the couple to be kissing, but they were sitting apart in total silence as though they had just had an argument. The man, in the driver's seat, was grey-haired and well-dressed. He was staring straight ahead of him, smoking a cigarette. The woman was much younger, with long brown hair and a heavy sheepskin coat. Her face was turned away from him, gazing out of the passenger-side window towards the wall of the yard.

Martin winked. Tess nodded and slipped around to the other side of the car. No midnight feast had ever been more eagerly anticipated than this one.

CHAPTER ELEVEN

The following morning was Sunday and Tess slept late. She slept so late that her father slipped into the room to check that she was all right before he went off to play a round of golf with a friend from the office.

'It's normal for a teenager,' her mother told him when he expressed concern. 'She'll be up and about soon.'

But when Tess had still not come downstairs by lunch-time, her mother made a cup of tea and brought it up to the bedroom. The first Tess knew of the day was the rattle of the runners on the curtain rail and the subsequent blaze of winter sunlight that fell upon her face. To her, still sleeping off the vampire feed of the night before, the sudden burst of light on her skin felt like a bucket of boiling water. She yelped and sat up, scrabbling for the bed covers.

'Tess!' said her mother. 'What on earth is wrong?'

Tess said nothing, but threw herself back down on the bed, pulling the duvet up over her head.

'Come on, Tess,' said her mother brightly. 'I've brought you a cup of tea.'

Tess's voice was muffled beneath the duvet. 'Leave me alone. I don't want to get up.'

'But it's one-thirty! If you don't get up soon you'll miss the daylight altogether!'

'What do I want with daylight?' Tess's voice sounded slightly husky to her mother.

'Are you ill, sweetheart? Have you got a sore throat?'

'No. I'm not ill. I just don't want to get up, all right?'

Her mother stayed in the room for another minute or two before deciding not to make an issue of it and returning downstairs. Tess listened to the receding footsteps, then turned over and tried to go back to sleep.

It was too late, though. She was awake now in a groggy, leaden sort of way. The events of the previous night slid into her mind, producing a strange mixture of guilt and delight. She knew that what had happened was wrong, but the memory of the hypnotic power of her vampire eyes and voice still thrilled her, and the sensation of that keen hunger being satisfied. She wondered where the couple from the car were now, and laughed out loud to think of them waking together and wondering how they had come to fall asleep in the first place. She thought of Martin sleeping in his blacked-out room and wondered whether she, like him, could get out of going to school.

Carefully, inch by inch, Tess drew the cover from her face. The light didn't feel so bad, now that the initial shock had passed. She reached for the cup of tea that her mother had left on the bedside table. As she sipped it, she ran her tongue around her mouth, feeling her teeth. They were neat and even again now, the canines back to their normal, blunt condition. But Tess's mind was still functioning along nocturnal lines, and it wasn't until daylight began to fade and her father returned from his game of golf that she finally dragged herself out of bed and went downstairs for a late, late breakfast.

'Anything special on at school, tomorrow, Tess?' said her father as they sat down to dinner that evening.

Tess had been withdrawn and sullen since she got up. At the best of times she got irritated by her parents' questions about school; now she saw this as a feeble attempt to draw her into a conversation that she didn't want.

'When is there ever anything special going on in school?' she answered, filling her mouth with roast beef.

Her father sighed and put down his knife and fork. Tess failed to heed the warning and reached out to turn the page of the magazine she had laid open beside her plate. He whipped it out from under her nose and flung it with a slap on to the floor. Tess's mother jumped at the uncharacteristic display of anger.

'I've had about enough of you, Tess,' he said. 'You mope around all day and treat your mother and myself as second-class citizens.'

Tess experienced a moment of anxiety. Her parents were so rarely critical that she hardly knew how to react. For a moment she was vulnerable, staring at the place where her magazine had been, struggling with shame. Then before she knew what was happening, the cold calm of her vampire mind came to her defence. Without looking up, she cut another forkful of beef.

'Do I?' she said.

'Yes, you do. You're doing it now.'

'Am I?'

Her father thumped the table with his fist, and Tess giggled inwardly at the sight of her mother jumping again, this time spilling her glass of water into her lap. But if her father noticed, he didn't pay any attention. He glared at Tess and said, 'I asked you a civil question and I expect a civil answer!'

'You asked me a boring question about a boring subject because you have a boring need to make boring conversation over dinner.'

Tess's words were met by a stunned silence.

'Boring dinner, I should have said,' she added, pushing a heap of mashed carrot and turnip towards the edge of her plate.

Her father stood up and pulled the plate away, knocking over his own glass of water in the process. Tess laughed as her mother leapt up and threw her already sodden napkin into the puddle. Then, slowly, she got to her feet and confronted her father. His face was stiff with fury.

'Until further notice,' he said, 'you are to stay in the house. I don't know who it is that you're meeting when you go out in the evenings, but whoever it is, they're clearly a bad influence on you.'

'Maybe,' said Tess. 'Or maybe I'm a bad influence on them. It all depends on which way you look at it, doesn't it?'

Her father stared at her, still unable to believe what he was hearing. Her mother was fussing with the highly-polished surface of the table, trying to pretend that nothing was happening while her life fell apart all around her.

'Get up to bed, young lady.'

'That's exactly where I was going.'

'And don't come down again until you're in a more reasonable humour, you understand?'

'Don't worry,' said Tess, heading towards the door. 'I won't come down until I'm Daddy's little darling again. Is that what you want?'

Her father's hands were clenched into fists, and they were shaking.

'Get out!' he yelled. 'Get out of my sight!'

Taking her time, Tess went out of the room and closed the door quietly behind her. Then, as an afterthought, she came back in, picked up her magazine from the floor and walked out.

Tess lay on her back on the bed in the darkness and stared up at the ceiling. Her father had been a fool to challenge her; there was no way he could win. As soon as he was asleep at night she would be gone, out of the window and away across the city, feeding herself with the best that Dublin could offer. And in the morning she wouldn't go down to breakfast even if he asked her; even if he begged her. What could he do? He couldn't force her to get up and go to school. She would lie in bed and sleep away the day, refusing to eat or drink. By the time a week had passed he would be putty in her hands; her mother, too. She would be like Martin: ruling the roost, getting whatever she wanted whenever she wanted it.

Tess smiled to herself in the darkness, then Switched and ran her tongue over her fangs. This was so easy, so perfect. She thought back over all her previous worries about what she was going to do when she reached fifteen. It all seemed so absurd now, and the answer so simple. It was good that she had met Martin and learned his secret. Perhaps she would meet him again tonight and hunt alongside him? But then again, perhaps not. They had no need of each other, after all, and the more she thought about hunting alone, the more she liked the idea.

Her mind stilled, alerted by soft footsteps on the stairs. Her mother, by the sound of it, coming to make her peace. Tess felt the familiar hunger and was surprised as the image of Martin's mother, pale and haggard, entered her mind. Of course! She smiled to herself, suddenly understanding the cause of the woman's mysterious anaemia.

The footsteps reached the top of the stairs and came on across the landing. Tess felt her mouth beginning to water at the prospect of an unexpected snack. Her mother was outside the door. The handle began to turn.

Not yet, though; not yet. Just in time, Tess got a grip on her vampire instincts. It was too early in the evening and too risky with her father in the house. Far better to wait for a more convenient occasion. Or an emergency, when other sources were hard to come by. Tonight, after all, she was eager for the hunt. There might well be times in the future when she felt more inclined to dine at home.

The light from the landing burst in and blinded Tess as the door opened. In the nick of time she Switched, keeping quite still as she did so, her face turned towards the wall.

'Tess?'

Her mother came cautiously into the room as though she was afraid that her daughter would pounce on her. Tess turned towards her, and watched as she picked up a chair and brought it over to the bedside.

'What's going on, Tess?' she said, sitting down in the chair and leaning forward with her elbows on her knees. The tone of concern in her voice almost disarmed Tess, but she recovered her guard just in time.

'Nothing's going on,' she said. 'Absolutely nothing.'

'Then why were you so unpleasant to your father?'

Tess sighed in exasperation, as though she was talking to an idiot. 'I wasn't rude to my father as a matter of fact,' she said. 'For the first time in my life I was honest with my father. It's the same every evening. He comes home from work and he says, "How was school, Tess?" "Did anything interesting happen in school today?" "Anything happening at school these days?" '

'But what's wrong with that?' said her mother.

'What's wrong with that is that he couldn't care less what's happening at school. If I told him the place burnt down and I carried the piano out on my back he'd just say, "That's good. What's for dinner?" '

'Oh, Tess. That's not fair.'

'It is fair. The truth is always fair.'

'And how do you come to be such an expert on the truth?' Her mother stood up and moved over to draw the curtains as she spoke.

'Leave them,' said Tess.

'I was just going to close them, that's all. Keep the heat in.'

'I like them open. Leave them.'

Tess's mother walked back to the chair, but she

didn't sit down. 'Now, you listen to me, Tess,' she began.

'I'm listening.'

'There's a possibility that you might be right about your father . . .'

'I am.'

'. . . Some of the time, that is. But as it happens, you were wrong today.'

'Oh?'

'Oh. Yes, oh. Your father has arranged to take the day off work tomorrow. He was about to ask you if it would be all right for you to take the day off school.'

Tess's eyes widened and she looked at her mother for the first time as she went on, 'He was planning for us all to get up at crack of dawn and go over to the zoo.'

'The zoo?'

'Yes. The zoo. There's going to be an awful crowd there tomorrow.' She paused, looking into Tess's blank face. 'Have you forgotten?'

'Forgotten what?'

'They're going to let the public in to see that bird they caught the other night.'

Tess sat up on the edge of the bed and stared into the middle distance. How could it have happened? How could she possibly have forgotten the phoenix? Not just for a few moments, but absolutely. She was quite certain that if her mother hadn't reminded her she would never have remembered it again. For the first time since she had assumed the vampire form, the horror of what she had done became clear to her. A desperate confusion flooded her mind as the phoenix memories returned and began to edge out the cold vampire complacency.

Her mother waited for a few moments, then said,

'Now. I've spoken to your father and he's still willing to go if you promise to think about your behaviour this evening. He doesn't want an apology: just a nice day out tomorrow and a bit more consideration in future. What do you say?'

Tess looked up, her face quite changed now. She nodded. 'I have to go,' she said.

'You don't have to,' said her mother, 'but it'd be a shame to miss the opportunity.'

Tess shook her head. 'I have to go,' she said again. Her mother put an arm around her shoulders and gave her a quick squeeze, then crossed the room towards the door. Tess found her shoes and began to put them on.

'And I will apologise,' she said.

As Tess watched TV with her parents that evening she had no awareness of what was going on beneath her. The city's rats, with Algernon somewhere among them, were digging, scratching, burrowing away, radiating outwards like the spokes of a wheel, still following their master's orders.

Most of the city underground had already been covered, since it had been dug up for foundations, and for sewerage, gas and electric systems. But directly beneath Tess's house, the rats were moving, breaking new ground as they pushed outwards into the unknown territory which lay beneath the park.

CHAPTER TWELVE

Before seven o'clock the following morning, Tess and her parents were standing outside the Dublin Zoo. Despite the early hour and the hard frost which had coated every leaf and blade of grass with silvery rime, there was already quite a queue of people there before them. The first ones in the line were wrapped in sleeping bags and blankets, and one or two gas stoves burned with yellow-blue flames beneath the street lights, brewing tea for cold campers.

Tess joined the line, pulling her pony tail out of the collar of her jacket and tightening the draw cords at her throat. Her father gave the pony tail an affectionate tug in an effort to break through the awkwardness which still lay between them. She gave him the best smile she could manage, but it wasn't great. Apart from anything else, Tess was desperately tired. She hadn't Switched at all the previous night; in her confusion she had decided to sleep on the problem in the hope that things would make more sense in the morning. But in the end she had found it impossible to sleep at all, and had spent the entire night in a terrible conflict with herself; swinging between her love for the phoenix and its ethereal existence and her desire for the bittersweet pleasures of the vampire. When her mother had come to call her at six-thirty, she had felt an enormous sense of relief, but it hadn't lasted long. Already the vampire side of her mind had begun to eat into her resolve to visit the phoenix. What was the point, after all? Why should she stand for hours in the freezing cold just for the sake of getting a glimpse of a namby-pamby bird that she had already seen?

The lights came on in the zoo, but there was still no sign of any activity at the gates. Tess shuddered as the frost bit deep into her tired bones. In an effort to close the contradictory voices out of her mind, she began to look around at the crowd. There were all kinds of people there, from new age 'crusties' with long-haired children to pin-striped businessmen who blew on their hands and stamped their polished brogues against the cold tarmac. The majority, though, seemed to be the type of people that Tess imagined would shoot birds rather than watch them; they wore waxed jackets or faded green anoraks with jeans and walking boots or green Wellingtons. The most noticeable thing about them was that they didn't seem to feel the cold as much as everyone else, but stood around in small groups chatting to each other as though they were quite accustomed to being out in the frost before dawn.

Tess examined the lines of parked cars and tried to match the people to their transport. There were a couple of brightly-coloured vans, a dormobile with dim lights on inside, several saloon cars with recent registration plates, a Morris Minor and four Land Rovers. As Tess watched, another one arrived, its diesel engine growling sweetly as it slowed and pulled into a space at the head of the line.

'I suppose it's too early to start on the breakfast?' said Tess's father.

'Of course it is,' said her mother. 'We've got three hours to wait before the gates open.'

'What do you think, Tess?' said her father, with a conspiratorial nudge of his elbow.

'I don't mind,' she said. She was still watching the Land Rover, expecting it to be loaded to the gills with Labrador dogs and men in deer-stalker hats.

'Just a cup of coffee?' said her father, in a wheedling voice.

The back door of the Land Rover opened and a huddle of children spilled out, stretching and yawning, their breath rising in misty clouds around them. The driver's door slammed and a man in a cloth cap walked around the bonnet, then went back to his own side to turn out the headlights.

Tess's mother conceded. 'All right. Just a small cup, though.'

The passenger door opened and swung back and forth on its hinges as a small figure manoeuvred around with considerable difficulty, until she was sitting sideways on the seat. The man in the cloth cap hurried round to help, and a moment later the elderly woman descended, stiffly but safely, on to the road.

Tess recognised her immediately. It was Lizzie, the eccentric old woman who had once been a Switcher herself, and had sent Tess and Kevin to the Arctic to do battle with the krools. Without thinking, Tess raced away from her parents and across the road, narrowly avoiding a minibus that was crawling along, looking for a space to park. Lizzie dropped her walking stick in surprise as Tess appeared at her side and flung her arms around her.

'Careful, girl! Careful of my old bones!' Lizzie suffered Tess's embrace for a moment or two, then extricated herself. 'This cold has me rusted up so I can hardly move!'

Tess stepped back and beamed at her friend. 'I never dreamt that you'd come,' she said. 'How did you know?'

'How did I know what?'

'How did you know that it was . . .' Tess stopped just in time, alerted by a fierce warning glint in Lizzie's eyes. The oldest of the four children, a girl of about nine, bent down to retrieve Lizzie's stick and handed it to her. The others stood in a shivering huddle on the road. Behind them, another Land Rover pulled up and waited for them to move.

But Lizzie was in no hurry. 'This is Mr Quinn, my neighbour,' she said. 'I told you about him, didn't I? He keeps his cattle on my land, and he helped me out that time when the weather was so bad. At least, some of the time.' She cast a surly glance at Mr Quinn, who cleared his throat and looked the other way. 'This here is Tessie,' Lizzie went on, 'who came snooping round my place last year with her young friend. What was his name again?'

'Kevin,' said Tess, nodding in greeting towards Mr Quinn. She was embarrassed now that her initial delight at seeing Lizzie had evaporated. Worse than that, she was unsure how she was going to explain the eccentric old woman to her parents.

'And as for how I knows,' Lizzie was saying,

looking pointedly at Tess, 'I read it in the newspapers like everyone else.'

Tess nodded, shamefaced. The driver of the waiting Land Rover honked his horn and the small group began to make their way towards the opposite pavement, all of them moving at a snail's pace to accommodate Lizzie's arthritis. Tess's mother was waiting for them on the footpath, and Tess cast around in her mind for some way of explaining Lizzie. There was no time to think, and she had to say something.

'Mother. This is Lizzie.'

The old woman stretched out a thin crooked hand, which Tess's mother accepted, a little reluctantly.

'Elizabeth Larkin,' said Lizzie, pompously, 'of Tibradden, County Dublin. I offered your daughter my hospitality during that cold snap we had that time.'

Tess's mother would never forget the 'cold snap', when her daughter had gone missing without warning and not returned until the thaw set in. Tess watched her face. She had never told her parents anything about what happened when she went away the previous year with Kevin, and they had never asked. She could see her mother's perplexity as she took in this information, knowing that it would do nothing to explain her disappearance but merely add to the mystery. Tess was afraid that she would ask Lizzie for more information but Lizzie was, as usual, a step ahead of her.

'This is my neighbour, Mr Quinn,' she said. 'He has most kindly brought me in to get a look at this funny pheasant, and I mustn't keep him waiting around. So nice to meet you.' With an authoritative air, Lizzie struck her cane on the frosty pavement and began to make her way towards the end of the rapidly lengthening queue.

Tess looked after them, surprised by the strength of her feelings for the old woman. When she had first seen her a few moments ago, she had felt that she had an ally, that she no longer had to face the current confusion alone. Now she wasn't so sure. Her heart was heavy as she and her mother made their way back to her father, who had stayed behind to hold their place.

'Who on earth was that?' he said.

'Lizzie. A mad old woman I met last year.'

'Where did you meet her? When?'

Tess was irritated by the questions. It hadn't been enough just to say hello to Lizzie. She badly wanted to talk to her. In the end it was her mother who had to fill the silence and answer her father's questions.

'She put Tess up during the snowstorms, apparently. Why didn't you tell us about her, Tess?'

Tess shrugged. Her parents looked at each other. Tess had always been secretive about her disappearance, and they had learnt not to pry. Nevertheless, the silence was full of tension. After a few minutes Tess said, 'Why don't you two have a cup of coffee? I fancy a wander around. I won't be long.'

Without waiting for a reply, she ducked out of the queue and made her way back along the side of the straggling crowds until she found Lizzie, standing a little to one side and leaning on her stick. People were streaming into the park now, some of them on foot, others in cars or coaches which pulled up beside the gates to unload. Tess was puzzled by the numbers. The capture of the bird had created a lot of publicity, but she wouldn't have expected so many people to turn out.

As though she were reading Tess's mind, Lizzie spoke.

'People is looking for something,' she said. 'There's nothing left to believe in, and people wants something new.'

Tess nodded, looking round at the faces in the crowd. There was something in what Lizzie had said; a deeper emotion than simple curiosity shone in the expressions of the people all around her. There was an eagerness, almost a hunger, to witness the mystery that was residing in the zoo buildings ahead.

Lizzie left firm instructions with the youngest of Mr Quinn's children to hold her place in the line. The child nodded, an expression of utter terror on her face. Her father ruffled her hair and offered to help with the job, and the child relaxed. Lizzie's body might have been old and frail, but she had a powerful personality and Tess could well understand how a small child might be intimidated by her. She smiled encouragingly and wondered, as she often did, whether that child had discovered the ability to Switch and, if she had, where it might lead her.

The sun was just rising as she and Lizzie made their slow way towards a stand of sycamore trees on the other side of the road. Sunlight might be beginning to overpower the streetlights, but it would be a long time before it made any significant impression on the crisp white frost underfoot.

'You's worried, girl,' said Lizzie as she propped herself carefully against the scaly trunk of one of the trees.

Tess sat down on a protruding root and nodded. 'Do you know who this bird is?' she said.

'Of course I do!' said Lizzie. 'He would have had something to answer for if he hadn't come to see me!'

'I suppose so,' said Tess, though somehow she couldn't imagine the phoenix answering to anyone, no matter what the call. 'The question is, though, how do we get him out of there?'

Lizzie nodded slowly and looked over towards the zoo. 'I suppose he has to come out, sooner or later.'

'But of course he has to come out! How could you think of leaving him in there?'

'Well, he can't come to any harm, can he? He'll always rise up again, won't he, whatever happens? He'll be rising up again after you and me and the zoo is long since gone and forgotten.'

'But he can't stay in captivity all his life! Or all his lives, whatever way you want to put it. And we've only got a week to get him out!'

'I wouldn't say it bothers him too much where he is,' said Lizzie. 'He is what he is; here, there, or anywhere else he might happen to be.'

Tess tried to resist what Lizzie was saying, but when she thought about it, she had to admit that it was true. The bliss of the phoenix existed in being, not in doing. Why should it matter to him where he was?

But Lizzie, true to form, had not finished confusing Tess yet.

'Still, he has to come out, all the same,' she was saying, 'though I isn't sure it'll be enough to make the difference.'

'Make what difference?'

Lizzie sighed and shifted uncomfortably. 'I's sure you knows already, girl, but if I has to explain it then I will. As best I can, that is.'

'Go on.'

'There is a great light in this city, and within the next hour or two people are going to be pouring in through these gates to see it. Every person who sees it is going to be affected by it. You mark my words: that bird in there will change people's lives.'

'Really?'

Lizzie nodded. 'For a while, anyway. But the truth about this world is that wherever there's light there has to be darkness, and as soon as that bird came into existence some nastiness was born to balance it out. What's more, I's as sure as I can be that where the evil is based isn't a million miles from here.'

She looked pointedly at Tess, who felt her mind cloud over with suspicion. What did the old woman know? What business was it of hers, anyway? For a moment the sunlight which was beginning to break through the branches overhead felt intolerable to her. Then, as quickly as it had come, the feeling passed away, leaving Tess in a turmoil of confusion.

'But what should I do, Lizzie?' she said, trying to hide the desperation which was edging into her voice. 'How do I choose?'

Lizzie shrugged. 'We all has to choose at some stage, girl,' she said. 'But it may not be as difficult as you thinks it is. Sometimes it isn't choices that is difficult, but the way we looks at them. It's not always what we are that needs changing, but the way we thinks. You know what I mean?'

'No!' said Tess. 'I have no idea what you mean.'

Lizzie was about to reply when her attention was caught by Tess's father running towards them across the grass.

'They've opened the gates early,' he called breathlessly. 'We'd better get back in line.'

Tess stood up and took Lizzie's elbow to help her

back to Mr Quinn and his family. She seemed to move infuriatingly slowly, and Tess could see her mother nearing the gate as the crowd flowed forward.

Lizzie stopped abruptly. Mr Quinn was making towards them across the road.

'You get along now, Tessie,' she said. 'And mind you take care, you hear?'

'Are you sure you'll be all right?'

'I'll be all right, and so will you if you takes care. I trusts you, girl. If you trusts yourself half as much, you'll know what to do when the time comes.'

She shook herself free of Tess's grasp and latched on to Mr Quinn. Tess wanted to hear more, but it was too late. Her father was moving in another direction, and was just about to be swallowed up by the crowd.

'That all sounded very serious and profound,' he said, as she caught up with him. 'Far too obscure for an old dunce like me. What was it all about, anyway?'

'I haven't the faintest idea,' said Tess, 'but I wish I had.'

CHAPTER THIRTEEN

'It must be because of all these people that they're opening early,' said Tess's mother as they approached the turnstiles. 'I'm sure the adverts said the zoo would open at ten.'

Tess looked back. The line stretched as far as she could see, back along the road between the zoo and the main gates of the park. A few gardai had arrived and were standing at intervals beside the queue, but so far there was no need for them; all was quiet and orderly.

Tess's father paid a harassed young woman in the nearest of the wooden kiosks at the gate, then grumbled about the price.

'Better be worth it. Awful lot of money just to look at one bird.'

'You can see all the rest of the animals as well if you want to,' said Tess.

'Leave him alone, Tess,' said her mother, good-naturedly. 'His life wouldn't be worth living if he couldn't find something to complain about.'

Once inside the zoo gates, there were several directions that a visitor could take, but not one person deviated from the line which dragged slowly on towards the centre of the compound. To Tess's surprise they passed by the aviary where she had used the pine marten's sharp wits to get a look at the phoenix, and headed on towards another building beside the café. It was a huge grey warehouse of a place with nothing in the way of architectural imagination to recommend it. Tess had been inside it once before, when it had housed a rather boring exhibition of model whales and dolphins. Now it had clearly been given over to displaying the phoenix. As they drew near, a man was in the process of changing the queuing time notice beside the door from 'two hours' to 'three hours'.

'Glad we got here early,' said Tess's mother. 'We'd have been waiting all day if we'd got up an hour later.'

Inside the entrance to the building a pair of uniformed security guards were making cursory checks of everyone's hand luggage. The family's picnic basket got a slightly more thorough examination before they were allowed to move on, and Tess noticed two or three shooting sticks leaning against the wall, waiting for their owners to reclaim them as they left.

'They're not taking any chances, are they?' said Tess's father as they moved forward with the crowd.

'I suppose that bird must be fairly valuable,' said her mother. 'It seems to be the only one of its kind.'

'We don't know that,' said Tess. 'I think it's ridiculous. Why couldn't they leave it alone to get on with its life? For all they know it might have a family somewhere.'

She peered around the side of a heavily-built man in front of her, but the crowd was still too thick to see anything. For a long time they didn't move at all, and the guard at the door had stopped any more people from coming in behind them. Then, after what seemed an age, the line began to dribble forward again.

The phoenix's cage was in the corner diagonally opposite to the entrance door. A wall of hardboard partitions ran down the centre of the building and prevented anyone seeing around the corner until they got there. The wait was infuriating; the long, slow crawl to that corner. But when they turned it, the endless queuing all seemed worthwhile.

The light hit them before they saw the bird itself, and it produced a powerful sensation. The glass-panelled cage was lit from above by a double row of fluorescent tubes, but the radiance that flooded out of that corner was far greater than what they could produce. Tess knew as soon as she saw the light that in some way or other, it was being produced by the bird itself. And its effect was extraordinary. The moment she came within its aura, and long before she saw the phoenix itself, Tess felt her mood shift; elevate, as though she had received some wonderful news or been given an unexpected gift. When the phoenix first appeared at her window she had felt like that, but she had assumed her joy came from knowing that Kevin had survived. Now she knew it was more than that. The bird had some sort of mystical power of its own, and as Tess looked around her in wonder she could see that it was affecting everyone in the building in the same way. There was still a certain amount of shoving going on behind them, but all those who had stepped into the light were completely at ease; in no hurry at all despite their proximity to the source of the light. Even the zoo staff, there to keep the visitors moving, were relaxed and smiling, in no hurry to move people along.

Tess giggled to herself, imagining the sign outside the door being changed again from 'three hours' to 'four hours', then from four to five, and five to six, as progress slowed to a contented standstill inside the building. She could visualise the crusties getting out their Jews' harps and bongo drums as they settled in for the day, and the waxed jackets and pin-stripes sitting down among them, clapping their hands and chanting.

But the line did eventually move on, slowly but surely, and a few minutes later the golden bird came into view. It sat on a solid wooden perch, suspended above a lush forest of green and red foliage growing from large pots on the gravel floor of the cage. The sight of that gravel, laid down above the compacted earth floor on which she and the other onlookers were standing, meant something to Tess, though at that moment she couldn't understand what. It seemed absurd to be noticing such details when the phoenix was sitting there in front of her in all his glory.

She fought down a sudden urge to Switch and join him there and then, to become a part of that glorious radiance that shone through the glass panels of the enclosure. Instead, she tried to catch the bird's eye, to let him know that she was there and had not abandoned him.

It wasn't easy. His gaze moved slowly and evenly

across the crowd, first one way and then the other. His expression was inscrutable and, when Tess did finally succeed in making contact with those calm, golden eyes, she could see no sign of recognition at all.

It disturbed her, and for a moment her buoyant mood deflated. Was she nothing to the phoenix? Was she just another pair of gawking eyes in the middle of this latest crop of uplifted faces? There was a certain arrogance about the bird's demeanour as he hung there above them all, passing his benevolent eyes from one to another, as distant as a priest handing out communion. The fat man moved sideways, blocking her view, and at the same time a sullen anger tugged at the edge of Tess's mind. If he was so detached, why shouldn't she be, too? Why should she care about him being stuck there for all eternity if he didn't even bother to acknowledge her presence? She could turn away now and never turn back, just slip off into the darkness of that other existence, to hunt the city streets in the hours of darkness and never be bothered with him again.

The crowd shuffled forward and she was edged along with them. The fat man stepped aside to get a better view and the light fell directly on Tess's face once again. As it did so, all thoughts of darkness were washed out of her mind and she was swept back into the jubilant mood of the encompassing gathering. The gaze of the phoenix passed over her again and she was perfect, glowing with an inner light as radiant as his own.

Outside the dull grey building, no one seemed in any hurry to move off towards their homes. If it hadn't been for the zoo officials who kept everyone moving along, people might have just sat down where they were, prepared to enjoy the weak winter sunshine for as long as it lasted. As it was, most people allowed themselves to be guided back to the gates, where a cordon of posts and plastic chains separated the exit from the dense crowds still coming in.

The grass was green again now, except for those shadowy places beneath the trees and hedges where the sun couldn't reach. Tess kept an eye out for Lizzie, but when she eventually spotted her a few metres from the entrance to the exhibition building, she was too far away to call out. She noticed the puzzled expressions on the faces of the incoming visitors as they observed those who were coming out, beaming with pleasure. In sudden excitement, Tess realised that something extraordinary was happening here. Whatever power the phoenix held within itself was infectious. People were being changed by it. It was pulling them out of their dull, everyday lives and inspiring them with some sort of new spirit.

As though he were echoing her thoughts, Tess's father suddenly stretched his arms up above his head as if he was trying to reach the sun and said, 'Do you know what?'

'What?' said Tess.

'I don't think I'll bother going on into the office after all. They can manage without me for one day. Let's go home and get the frisbee, then find a quiet spot somewhere and have our breakfast.'

'Does that mean I can stay off school, then?'

Her mother laughed, her voice bubbling with the same inner excitement that everyone seemed to be feeling. 'We may be in a good mood,' she said, 'but we'd hardly go as far as playing frisbee without you!'

★

'Oh, wouldn't you?' Tess thought to herself as she sprawled luxuriously among the remains of their picnic breakfast an hour later. Her parents were playing frisbee some distance away, fooling about like young children in the sun. She was about to get up and join them when she noticed a familiar group of people making their way towards her across the park. It was Lizzie, with her escort of Mr Quinn and his children. As she stood up to go and meet them, Tess saw Lizzie turn to the others and give them some sort of command. They dropped back and sat down on the grass to wait for her, while she came on alone.

Tess bounced over to her, eager as a puppy, but something in Lizzie's expression made her hesitate. The old woman looked marvellous, as though she was twenty years younger. Even her stiffness had eased, and she hardly used her cane at all as she came forward to meet Tess. But there was something in her eyes apart from the reflected glow of the phoenix's radiance. It was clear to Tess that Lizzie had something on her mind.

'Well, young lady?' she said as Tess approached. 'What does you think of all that?'

'Oh, Lizzie. It's wonderful, isn't it?'

'Oh, it's wonderful, all right. Of course it's wonderful. Look at all these people all over the place, wonderfulling away the day.'

Tess looked round at the growing crowds enjoying the space and the fresh air of the park. The grass was becoming almost crowded as people continued to file in and out of the zoo, and swelled the numbers lying about under the sun.

'Well? What's wrong with that?'

'There's nothing wrong with that, unless someone has work to do.'

'Oh, come on, Lizzie! I didn't think that you were the sort to get wound up over a few people taking a day off work!'

'I isn't talking about that lot!' said Lizzie, sounding exasperated. 'I's talking about you!'

'Me! But you're the one who goes on about young people filling their heads up with useless rubbish and having no room left for what they need to know. How can you turn round and object to me taking a day off school?'

As she was speaking, Tess noticed Lizzie glancing past her and turning slightly away. 'Don't look now,' she said with a nonchalant kind of expression, 'but here comes trouble.' She lowered her voice and spoke rapidly, determined to say what she had to before they were interrupted. 'I isn't talking about school, you little fool. I's talking about work. Real work. You's here lounging around in the sun, lapping up all this light everywhere like a cat laps up cream . . .' Her voice lowered even further and Tess glanced round to see her parents approaching, their faces beaming with welcome.

'You has to do something with it!' Lizzie hissed. 'You's wasting time and you's wasting what that bird has given you! You has work to do.'

'Hello again,' said Tess's father breezily, extending a warm, ruddy hand towards Lizzie. 'I'm glad you found us. I was hoping to get a word with you.'

'How do you do, Mrs Larkin?' said Tess's mother, smiling from ear to ear.

'I's doing fine, thanks, Mrs. And how's you doing yourself? I's sorry I hasn't time to be standing around and chatting, but Mr Quinn there is a busy farmer, and he's waiting to drive me back to Tibradden. You's most welcome to call if you's in the locality.'

Before Tess's parents had a chance to reply, Lizzie had turned on her heel and begun to walk back across the park.

CHAPTER FOURTEEN

Tess's parents watched with benign expressions as Lizzie and the Quinns departed. To their euphoric minds Lizzie's behaviour was quite forgivable, no more than mildly eccentric. For Tess, however, the aspect of the day had changed entirely. She knew in her heart that Lizzie was right. There was something she ought to be doing. The problem was, she couldn't think what it was.

'Come on,' said her father, 'where's that frisbee?'

Frisbee would be fun, even though she was no good at it. But playing frisbee wasn't what she ought to be doing. She scanned the horizon of the park, looking for clues. For the most part, her view was blocked by trees, but here and there the buildings of the city showed through or above them.

'Catch, Tess!'

She swung round, just in time to see the bright-green frisbee go sailing over her head and disappear among the branches of a copse which stood in a hollow some distance away. It was a mighty throw, and the wind had caught it as well. Tess watched as her parents raced past in pursuit and began hunting through the dead grass beneath the trees. She went over and began to help in the search, but her attention was taken by a number of small, neat piles of earth which were spread around the area. They were like molehills, but Tess knew there weren't any moles in Ireland. Everything today had a strange, dreamlike quality and Tess tried to concentrate; tried to make sense of what was going on. She might have found the scene humorous if it hadn't been for the persistent nagging from the back of her mind about the task that awaited her.

The first time the idea came to her she disliked it so much that she ignored it. Coming back a second time with the ring of truth, it wasn't so easily put aside. She tried to reason the thought away, was still trying as her parents gave up and came back to her side.

'No use,' said her mother. 'It seems to be lost.'

'Sorry about that,' said Tess.

'No, no,' said her father. 'It was way, way too high. There was no way you could have caught it.'

'Did you notice the molehills?'

'Molehills? But there aren't any moles in Ireland!'

The idea came back and Tess finally accepted it. 'Never mind,' she said. 'I was thinking of paying a visit to someone. Would that be OK?'

'Who is it?'

'A friend of mine called Martin. He's off school these days.'

'Is he sick?'

'Yes, he is. Sort of.' As she said it, Tess realised

that this wasn't a lie. From her current viewpoint, out here under a cloudless sky and filled with the vibrancy of life, anyone who chose to spend their days sleeping behind closed curtains had to be sick.

Tess's father looked slightly disappointed, but he was far too happy to remain so for long.

'Don't be too late back,' was all he said.

It was early afternoon as Tess walked down the narrow street in Phibsboro. The sun was still shining, but apart from a shallow strip of brightness on the opposite pavement, the street was covered in shadows cast by the surrounding houses. Frost still lay in some of the remoter corners of the small front gardens and Tess shivered as she made her way up to Martin's front door.

As before, her knock was followed by a long silence. She waited, half hoping that no one would come and she could return to the sanctity of the park with a clear conscience. But Martin's mother did come, eventually, from some dreary corner of the house that Tess chose not to imagine.

Her face brightened when she saw Tess standing at the door, but not enough to bring colour to the pasty skin.

'Hello?' she said. 'Have you come to visit Martin again?'

'Yes. Is he in?'

His mother's face clouded over again. 'Where else would he be?' She glanced around at the stairs and then, to Tess's surprise, stepped out of the house and joined her on the front step, pulling the door to behind her.

'I probably shouldn't tell you this,' she said, leaning close to Tess and speaking in a low voice, 'but we had the social worker here this morning. She went up and talked to himself in the bed, but she didn't get much sense out of him. When she came down she told me that if he didn't start going back to school soon he'd be taken away from me and put into Borstal. Something like that, anyway.'

She looked at Tess closely for a reaction. Tess tried to ignore the smell of cheap margarine that lingered on the woman's clothes, and put on several expressions, one after another. She started with dismay first, then sympathy, then disapproval, but none of them really worked very well because all she could honestly think was that it would be a waste of everyone's time. She seemed to have done something right, though, because Martin's mother nodded gravely and went on, 'I don't know what's wrong with the boy. He hasn't been the same since his father died.'

'His father died?'

'Didn't you know that? I thought everyone must know. It affected him very badly, right from the start. He never cried, not once. He just seemed to close down like a clam. I suppose I should have taken more notice at the time, but I always thought that he would be all right in the end.'

She paused and listened at the crack in the front door for a minute before continuing, 'I've tried everything. Everything. I've done the rounds of the town with him; taken him to every counsellor and psychiatrist and psychologist in the phone book. He won't take any notice of them, though. He goes once and makes a fool of them, then refuses to go to any more appointments.'

Tess nodded, trying to look sage and concerned. Martin's mother sighed.

'The fact is, I'm at my wits' end. My own health isn't the best and I'm worn out trying to cope. But I don't want them to take him away. He may not be perfect but he's all I've got.'

She looked into the middle distance, her eyes glossing over with distress. For a long time she stood quite still, while Tess grew colder and colder and felt more and more awkward; then, at last, she seemed to pull herself together.

'I'm glad you've come again,' she said. 'I have to admit that I didn't think you would, but I'm glad you did. Martin seems to like you. He was quite cheerful for a while after your last visit. I don't suppose . . .' She stopped, looking searchingly at Tess as though she wasn't sure whether she could trust her or not.

'You don't suppose what?'

The woman sighed, her deathly white face relaxing into its usual defeated slackness. 'I don't suppose you'd talk to him? Try and make him see reason?'

Tess looked away. There was no point in trying to explain that she had come with exactly that purpose in mind. 'I'll do my best,' she said. 'But I wouldn't raise your hopes too high if I were you.'

In the stuffy darkness of Martin's room, his hands and face showed up against the bedclothes like pale moths in the night. In the corner opposite, the greeny-blue light on the video clock flashed on and off: 00.00. 00.00. The curtains had been reinforced by a grey army blanket so that the only light coming in from the day was a feeble line of paler grey above the curtain rod.

Tess waited in the doorway until her eyes became accustomed to the gloom and she could hear Martin's slow, regular breathing, then she crossed over to the bedside. The boy's face wore a smug, satisfied expression and the hairs on the back of Tess's neck prickled as she became aware once again of the dark power which slumbered within that innocuous frame. But she had power as well: the inner freedom that the phoenix had given her. That was why Lizzie had been so keen for her to come soon, before it wore off. If she couldn't stand up to him, who could?

She called to him, gently. He stirred and sucked his teeth but didn't wake. She called again, a little louder. He sighed and woke, his eyes searching the room until they found her face. For a moment he looked bewildered, as though her presence there didn't fit with the dreams he had been having. Then he recovered his confidence, smiled his sweet smile and sat up.

Tess smiled back. 'Sorry to wake you. But it's a beautiful day outside.'

'Is it?' Martin yawned and stretched. Tess moved over towards the window, but he said, 'Whoa, hold on. One step at a time, eh?'

He reached out and switched on a heavily-shaded lamp which stood on the bedside table, then he leaned back and stretched himself again.

Tess cleared a chair and pulled it up beside his feet. 'Your mother's bringing us breakfast,' she said. 'Well, lunch, actually.'

Martin laughed and rubbed his bleary eyes. 'I was out until nearly dawn, but the pickings were mean. I hope she's making a fry.'

Tess made no answer and there was an awkward silence for a few minutes. Then Martin sighed and cuddled himself back down into the bedclothes.

Tess looked over at the mop of red hair which

shaded his marble-green eyes and felt a sudden surge of affection for him. He couldn't be that bad, he just couldn't. He was only a boy, after all.

'You didn't tell me that your father died,' she said.

Martin shrugged, pulling the covers tight for a moment over his toes. 'Did my mother tell you that?'

'Yes. Just now. Downstairs.'

'She tells everyone about it. She thinks it's like, some kind of big tragedy in my life which made me go wrong. She thinks it explains everything, but it doesn't. It doesn't explain anything. It didn't make any difference to me at all.'

'I find that hard to believe. How could you lose your father and not be affected by it?'

'How could *you*, you mean?' Martin's voice had a sharp edge that Tess hadn't heard before. 'You're talking about yourself,' he went on, 'not about me. Everyone does that. You'd miss your father so you assume everyone else would, too. But I didn't, not one bit. I didn't miss him 'cos I hated him.'

His face wore a sullen, bitter expression as he spoke, and his eyes were like glinting granite when he turned to Tess and said, 'Do you understand?'

Tess kept her face straight, determined to hide the unease his words had produced in her heart. 'Not really,' she said.

'Do you want me to tell you about it?'

'If you want to.'

'It's very gory. Do you like gory stories?'

Tess shrugged, torn between ghoulish curiosity and what she liked to think of as her finer sensibilities. 'I don't mind.'

'No, I'm sure you don't.' Martin's tone was sarcastic. 'But I'll tell you anyway. I like talking about it. I've talked about it to every shrink in Dublin, so it doesn't bother me one bit.'

He stopped, listening. There were slow footsteps on the stairs, and a moment later his mother elbowed the door open, struggling beneath the weight of a heavily-laden tray. Tess jumped up and unloaded the plates, then, while Martin's mother got her breath back, reloaded the tray with yesterday's empty cups and dishes.

'I'll bring it down for you,' she said.

'No. You stay here and have your chat. If you need anything else, give me a shout, all right?'

When his mother was gone, Martin began tucking into his plate of rashers and black pudding.

'We used to live in the countryside, you know. Just outside Dublin.'

'Did you?' Tess thought he had changed the subject, but he went on, 'Yes. We had a run-down old cottage and a few acres. My dad used to breed greyhounds and sell them to people from England. That was all he thought about: greyhounds, greyhounds and greyhounds.'

He paused for a minute to chew, then went on. 'It was a weird kind of life. One minute we'd be living on bread and margarine, wondering how we were going to last another week, and the next thing, he'd sell a dog or a pup for silly money to some English trainer and we'd be rolling in it. New clothes for me and my mother, Chinese takeaways every night of the week, him off to the pub buying rounds for the parish. Then back to bread and margarine again. I didn't mind, though. At least it was exciting.'

Tess poured out tea and handed him a cup. He took a few sips, then perched it on the bedside table beside the lamp and returned to the fry.

'Then what?' said Tess.

'Where was I? Oh, yes. I was into top gear by that time with this animal thing. What did you call us? Switchers, that's right. Well I used to be off in the woods and fields every spare minute trying out all kinds of things. I suppose it was good while it lasted. Then one of our neighbours gave me a donkey foal. Have you ever seen one?'

'Only in the zoo.'

'Yeah. Not many people keep donkeys these days. But the foal was . . .' He felt silent, staring ahead of him, and for a moment Tess fancied that he was vulnerable, that his guard had finally dropped. But if it had, it wasn't for long.

'Fact was that I was dead soft in those days. I doted on that little donkey like a right eejit. Spent half my time out in the shed with it, sometimes being another donkey, sometimes just being myself.'

'Bet you didn't tell that to the shrinks.'

Martin laughed. 'Be a lot more probable than some of the things I did tell them. They wouldn't know the difference anyhow. I didn't meet a single one who was the full shilling. I don't know how they're supposed to cure anyone else.'

He gave his full attention to his breakfast until Tess said, 'Go on. About the donkey.'

'There's not much to tell. Except that my dad said we had to get rid of her.'

'Why?'

'He said he needed the shed for his hounds. And she couldn't live out on the land because he sold the hay every year and then exercised the dogs there. He said I could have a pup from the next litter instead of the donkey and it would be worth twenty times

112

what she was, but that wasn't the point. Not then, anyway.'

Martin stopped to finish his breakfast. Outside, the birds were beginning to tune down as the short day drew towards an end, and Tess wished that she could see a last glimpse of sunshine. She looked over at the curtains, then decided against it, unwilling to disturb the atmosphere.

Martin wiped up the last of the grease with a piece of soggy toast, then put his plate down beside the bed, balancing it on his upturned trainers.

'So, anyway,' he said, wiping his mouth on the hem of his T-shirt, 'one evening my dad borrowed a cattle trailer and we brought the donkey out to some friends of his in Naas. Fifteen quid is all they gave me for her. It wasn't that, though. I didn't care about the money. The worst thing was that they had grey-hounds, too, and I was sure they only wanted my donkey for dog food.

'I wouldn't care now, but it bothered me then. There was nothing I could do about it, you see. I felt completely helpless. And then they got down the bottle of whisky and my dad sat there the whole evening drinking and laughing his head off. Have you seen people get drunk? Have you seen how stupid they look, and how clever they think they are?' Martin's sour expression accentuated the anger he was feeling. 'I hated him. I hated him so much I wished he was dead.'

He gulped down his tea and held the cup out to Tess for a refill. 'Ready for the gory bit?'

She nodded, putting aside her half-eaten fry. Martin's face held a strange kind of delight as he started up with his story again.

'It was pitch-dark when we started home that

113

night, and there was only one headlight working on the van. My dad took the back roads home because he didn't want to run into the cops with all that drink in him. He was driving too fast, as usual. I always wore my seat belt when he was driving, never with my ma. He didn't wear his, specially since they brought in the law that said you had to. He wasn't a violent man, but he'd go out of his way to get on the wrong side of the law if he could. That was just the way he was.

'So when this black cow appeared in the middle of the road, he didn't have a chance. I don't remember hitting her. I just remember seeing her on the road, coming out of nowhere, then waking up in the van with blood all over the place.'

Martin looked over to check Tess's reaction, but she was giving nothing away.

'I didn't know if the blood belonged to Dad or to the cow, and to tell you the truth I didn't care. The van was on its side in the ditch, and Dad's door had swung open during the crash and bent double under the wing. That was how the light came to be on inside the cab and I could see all the blood. Dad was covered in it and he wasn't moving. I was hanging over him, caught in the seat belt. All I could think of was getting out. I didn't care what had happened to him. I was really cool and calculated, manoeuvring myself around so that I could get a foot on the gear housing and lever myself out without standing on him. In the end I managed it. Then I just stood on the road for ages – hours, maybe – watching this sticky mess of a cow thrashing about on the road. And all I could think was that I didn't care. I had wished he was dead and now I didn't care whether he was or not. I knew then that I was a bad lot; always had been, always will be.'

'I don't believe that,' said Tess.

'Then you're a fool,' said Martin. He looked straight at her, the cold shadow of his night-time self at the forefront of his eyes. 'After it happened my mother couldn't bear to live out there any more. She sold the house and the land; turned out to be worth a fortune as a development site. We moved here. Too soon, perhaps, some of the shrinks said. I didn't speak to anyone for weeks, maybe months. I do now, though. I'll talk to anyone who wants to listen to me. Why not? It makes no difference. No one can touch me.'

Tess could think of nothing to say. For a long time they sat in silence until at last the gloom became too much for Tess.

'Can I open the curtains now? At least take a look at the day before it gets dark?'

Martin nodded. 'I was waiting for you last night,' he said. 'Where did you get to?'

Tess shrugged and went over to the window. 'Nowhere in particular. I went to sleep. Had to get up early this morning to go and see the phoenix in the zoo.'

'Oh, yes. Your phoenix. I keep forgetting about him.' Martin winced as Tess began to dismantle the blanket barricade and daylight lunged into the room. 'How is he?'

'He's . . .' Tess dried up, lost for words which would describe the glorious experience of the morning. 'He's perfect,' was all she could think of.

'That's good,' said Martin.

'But you should go and see for yourself. We haven't got all that much time; they're planning to move him to America at the end of the week, so you'd better go as soon as you can. There's an awful crush there at the moment, but if we got up really early in the morning . . .'

Martin cut across her words. 'Naa. I don't think I'll bother.'

It was the first direct blow, and Tess felt her sense of well-being begin to diminish. She turned, her back to the window. 'What do you mean, you won't bother?'

Martin's face was screwed up against the light at Tess's back. 'I won't bother,' he said again. 'Why should I?'

'Why should you?' said Tess. 'Well, there's two reasons, actually. One is that the phoenix is probably the most beautiful thing you'll ever see. It'll change your life, I guarantee it.'

Martin nodded complacently. 'And the other reason?'

'The other is that you promised me you'd help me get him out. You have to come and look at where he is, so we can work out a plan.'

Martin shook his head with an expression of disdain. 'I didn't promise you anything.'

'Yes you did. You said that you'd help me if I tried your way first. I did that; I kept my side of the bargain. Now it's your turn.'

But again the boy shook his head. 'I didn't promise anything. I said that I might consider it, that's all. And I still might.'

Tess waited expectantly as Martin swung his legs out of the bed and stood up, taking his time.

'But I won't,' he said.

It was like being kicked in the teeth. Tess turned away to hide the fury that was rising like a rush of blood to her face. The phoenix light within her was eclipsed by that rage, and she floundered between enemies, one without, the other within. He was playing with her, teasing her, that was all. He had never had any intention of coming towards her way of seeing things; not one single step.

CHAPTER FIFTEEN

Tess couldn't face Martin's mother now that she had failed so miserably in her mission. Instead she slipped quietly down the stairs, out of the front door and away down the street.

The last of the sunlight held no warmth, but it had that sweet, golden hue of evening which made it seem more substantial than it had been earlier in the day. Tess was reminded of the light emitted by the phoenix, and she tried to settle her thoughts and recapture her earlier mood.

She had left Martin's house in a hurry, not because she was afraid of him but because she was afraid that her own feelings of anger and betrayal would overwhelm her. As she warmed to the stroll through the darkening streets, the strange contradictions of her situation began to become apparent to her. She was being swung like a pendulum between two opposing forces, one dark and bent upon nothing more than satisfying its own desires, the other light, peaceful, beyond human yearnings and frailties. The first saw itself as all-important, with others being no more than a means of satisfying its needs, while the second had no need of others, but was perfect within itself. The choice ought to have been simple, according to the morality that Tess had been taught both at home and at school, but when faced with those opposites in reality, was far from being so. Because the phoenix, for all its light-giving qualities, was powerless when faced with opposition. How otherwise could it be caught so easily and held captive, at the mercy of those who held the keys? It might continue; it might rise again from its own ashes, and again, and again. But what use was that if it couldn't move about freely and spread its influence?

The vampire, on the other hand, would always be free to stalk the earth, even if it was restricted to the hours of darkness. It had the power to mesmerise, to bring others under its control. And in a confrontation, as Tess had found out, the only defence that existed against the creature was to become as he was. This had happened to her in the street under the trees, and in a slightly different way it had just happened again. The only response Tess had found to Martin's coldness was a coldness of her own, despite all her good intentions. Under threat, the phoenix force had diminished and the vampire force had grown.

Tess tried to remember what Lizzie had said. 'It's not what we are that needs changing but what we thinks.' Was that it? In any event, the words made no sense. Tess felt as though the seams of her mind were about to give way under the stress of the inner conflict. She wished that she had never met Martin, or Kevin either. She wished, for the first time in her life, that she had never discovered her power to Switch and that she was safely on the course that her parents wanted for her; towards a good education and a secure job. Life would be so simple, then; the only choices she would be faced with would be her Leaving Cert subjects.

She felt like screaming and began to run, trying to drown out the pursuing voices, both the light and the dark. When she got back to the house she barely greeted her mother, who was frying burgers in the kitchen, but went straight through to the sitting room and turned on the TV. A children's programme was on; it seemed fatuous, but lulled her like an old song and, exhausted from the excitement of the day and from lack of sleep, Tess dozed off.

She dreamt that the room was full of rats, a moving carpet of silky grey-brown. The rats were trying to get her attention, sending out strange picture calls, but she was refusing to listen. They were becoming more and more agitated, and some of them had begun to climb up on to her bed.

She woke and opened her eyes on to darkness. For a moment she didn't know where she was, then the familiar shape of the bay window reminded her that she had fallen asleep in the sitting room. One or other of her parents had brought down her duvet and pillow; she was snug and warm, wrapped up on the settee. She glanced at the luminous hands of her watch. Three a.m. With a sense of relief, she turned round to go back to sleep.

Something wriggled on the settee beside her. At the same time, something small and heavy ran across the top of the duvet. This was no dream. Tess threw off the cover and sat up, reaching out blindly for the switch of the standing lamp beside the settee. In the dim orange glow cast from the street lights outside the window, she could see her duvet moving on the floor as the rats beneath it squirmed around, looking for a way out. As her initial terror passed off, Tess relaxed, and was immediately bombarded by rat minds throwing images at her. It hadn't been a dream. The rats had come, and they had brought a message from their master.

For a long moment, Tess considered refusing his demand. She was afraid of what she might discover; afraid of the vampire's night-time power. But something stronger than fear lured her. Whatever her final decision might be, she needed to know everything there was to know.

She reassured the clamorous rats and sat for a while trying to compose herself; trying, without success, to draw upon the residual serenity somewhere within. She failed to find it, but discovered instead a small corner of her heart which still hoped to save not only herself, but Martin as well, from the eternal alienation of a vampire existence.

Despite the anxiety which wrenched at her guts there was no question of changing her mind. She took a deep breath and Switched, hating the transition as always but welcoming the alertness of the rat, and the vibrant certainty of its being.

The others led the way. There must have been about fifty of them, steaming down through a hole in the floorboards that Tess was sure wasn't there yesterday. One by one they dropped down through the joists beneath the floor and on to the uneven, muddy shale of the foundations. It was the last bit of open space that they were to see for quite a while, for the next minute they were underground, racing nose-to-tail through a newly-dug tunnel.

It was more like something a mole would dig than a rat and Tess remembered the little piles of earth she had seen in the park. Here was the answer to that mystery, at least. The earth that had been excavated would have to have been put somewhere. Below ground, the tunnels were economical, just wide enough for a rat to pass through at full stretch with no concession made for whiskers. Every few feet, subsidiary tunnels branched off the main one; some going up, some going down, some heading off on the same level, at right angles. As they sped along, the rats explained the system to Tess; how it had been devised so that every patch of ground beneath the city and the park could be searched. They would not, however, describe for her what they had found, despite their obvious excitement.

For the most part, the journey was easy going, if a little dull and claustrophobic. But on two occasions the entire party was brought to a halt by subsidence in the tunnel ahead. When that happened, the lead rat had to dig a way through, passing the fallen earth back from rat to rat until it reached the end of the line or the entrance to an excavation tunnel, whichever came first. The delays only served to heighten Tess's sense of expectation, so that by the time they eventually arrived at their destination, about half a mile from the edge of the park, she was bursting with curiosity.

The first she knew of their impending arrival was when the file turned in to a subsidiary tunnel on the right-hand side. It ran along straight for a few yards, and a single tip-head passage forked off to the left, sloping gradually upwards. Soon afterwards, the route began to slope downwards, gently at first, then more sharply. The earth was quite wet at that depth and the tunnel, which was clearly well-used, had turned into a mud-slide. The rats at the front tried to use outstretched paws to brake their descent, but the pressure of those careering down behind added to their speed, so that when they reached their destination they went shooting out into space like champagne corks.

Rats are hardy creatures, however, and take no notice of the occasional tumble. One by one they picked themselves up, licked their paws, polished their whiskers and were ready for action again.

And there was plenty of it. It was pitch dark down there beneath the ground, but between the sounds she could hear and the images she picked up from the minds of the other rats, Tess was able to get a fairly clear picture of what was going on.

They were in an underground chamber of some kind. Parts of the roof were still held up by pillars which supported crossed arches, but in other places these had given way and the chamber had filled with earth and rubble. Tree roots had reached down into the cavity, and one of the predominant sounds was of rats' teeth, gnawing through them to clear them away.

It was clear to Tess's human mind that this must have been the crypt of some long-forgotten church which had once stood above it. It was a dramatic find. Tess was sure that no one knew the place existed. Her human mind was aware of a brief thrill of excitement before the realisation of what she was here for sank home. There were two or three stone tombs in the chamber. One of them was standing in the open, the others were half buried by the subsidence of the roof. The rats were busy digging them out. Earth and small stones were flying everywhere, and the rats swore at each other a great deal as they got pelted by the debris. But despite this, the work was progressing at good speed.

Tess knew now that it wasn't treasure Martin was looking for. She knew as well that, despite what he had said, he hadn't the slightest interest in archaeology. She was just arriving at the obvious conclusion when a large shape appeared from nowhere, right there beside her. It made huge, hollow sounds with no meaning at all, and the rats' first instinct was to leap for the tunnels, which caused a great deal of useless falling around the place. The truth dawned on all their minds at the same moment. Their master had been among them for a while in rat form. Now he had assumed his own shape and was talking into the darkness in a language the rats didn't understand. They sniffed the air for a while, twitching their whiskers and passing information backwards and forwards to each other. Then, as though of one mind, they started back to work again.

Tess stayed where she was, close to the base of one of the great stone tombs. She could sense the vampire's mind trying to search her out, and shielded herself as well as she could. She needed time to decide what to do.

One or two of the nearer rats sensed Tess's fear and asked her what the problem was. She shut out their communications and tried to concentrate. What was she going to do? The only way out was back along the rat tunnels and Tess had a dreadful feeling that if she tried to go against the tide she would meet with little sympathy from the other rats. No other alternative seemed to offer any better chance. If she became a phoenix she could flood the crypt with light, might possibly even succeed in driving the vampire back into rat form and away down the tunnels, but it would not be a permanent solution to anything. Sooner or later she would have to find a way out, and when she did they'd be waiting for her.

The vampire mind was beginning to exert irresistible pressure upon her weak rat personality. Tess Switched quickly, before she lost the initiative, and found herself human again. There seemed to be no other choice, and at least this way she could think straight.

Or so she hoped. Without the extra nocturnal senses of the rat, Tess was helpless there beneath the ground. The darkness was total; silent for a moment as the rats adjusted to her altered presence, then full of their unseen scuffling and scratching. And, worse than that, there was someone in the enclosed space who was watching her without being seen.

'Where are you?' she said to the darkness. There was no answer, and if someone was breathing, the sound was lost behind the restless activity of the rats. Tess had never known claustrophobia before. She experienced it now: a brief, breathless panic at being enclosed on all sides. But the feeling didn't last long. A moment later it was replaced by sheer terror as she thought about the being that was closed in there with her. In that minute, her body seemed to become dysfunctional, as rigid and useless as a Cindy doll propped up against the cold stone wall.

She had been wrong about thinking straight. The truth was that she couldn't think at all. A low snigger slid out of the darkness, but she couldn't tell where it came from. Tess's fear suddenly converted into fury and, completely without thinking, she let fly with a series of the foulest swear-words she had ever heard.

The reply was another mocking laugh. All around them the rats continued working in the darkness.

'What are you afraid of?' said the vampire, his voice like poisoned syrup.

'What do you think I'm afraid of?' Tess was still shouting, her voice ringing back at her from the cold stone and damp earth. For an instant she wondered if she could be heard above the ground. There might be people around the park, sleeping overnight perhaps, to be early in tomorrow's queue to see the phoenix.

'But you have nothing to be afraid of, Tess.' The rich voice was amplified somehow by the enclosed space so that it seemed to be coming from all directions at once.

'Not much, I don't.' Tess jumped as a pebble flicked out by the eager digging of one of the rats bounced off her temple. She took a deep breath, aware of a trembling throughout her whole body. 'You're doing what you did before, aren't you?'

'What did I do before?'

'In the street the other day. You've got me trapped into a corner so that I'll have to Switch and become like you.'

The air seemed to be getting thinner. It smelled of rats and of ancient corruption. For the first time Tess thought of the original function of these tombs. She shuddered, and a new determination entered her heart. 'I won't, though,' she said. 'I have more tricks up my sleeve than you could imagine.'

It was a lie. Tess hadn't the faintest idea how to get out of this one, but her words seemed to have some effect, because the vampire fell silent for a while.

A rat scuttled over her foot. In the reprieve, she reached out with her rat mind to talk to it, and to her surprise a familiar signature of baby images came back. It was Algernon, camouflaged by the darkness; just another of the guys. Her mind flowed out to him, filled with relief at meeting someone familiar in this ordeal. Algernon's baby-talk returned; he was exhausted but proud of himself to be here working for the master. Reaching down to her feet, she found his little form beside her shoe. She closed her hands around him, anticipating his warmth against her face and neck, the pleasure of pets, the giving and receiving of comfort. But this new Algernon was no one's pet. He jerked wildly and jack-knifed in her hands, swivelling his head round and sinking his teeth deep into the flesh of her hand. Tess cried out and whipped her hand away, flinging Algernon out into the darkness in an automatic reaction. Straightening up, she felt the damp wall behind her again. Algernon's allegiance had changed. There was no comfort to be found in this place.

The shock of the betrayal seemed to deprive Tess of the last of her energy. Her breathing had become rapid and shallow as though there wasn't enough oxygen in the fetid atmosphere. She wondered briefly whether or not the vampire needed air and decided that he probably didn't. Nothing down here in the darkness seemed to be in her favour.

There was a flurry of squeaks as a fall of fresh earth and stones sent a party of miners scattering in all directions. In the relative silence that followed before they started work again, Tess came close to panic, gripped by a vision of the whole place caving in and burying her alive.

Martin's cold voice shifted her attention. 'Do you know what we're doing here, Tess?'

'Overseeing your archaeological dig, I suppose.' At the back of her mind, Tess knew much more, but the idea wouldn't come forward. It refused to be put into words.

'Yes. But do you know why?'

The understanding niggled its way out and, in a ghastly moment of realisation, Tess did know. He must have seen the expression on her face, even though she couldn't see him, because he said, 'Don't be so shocked. Everyone needs a place to sleep, after all.'

It was always the way, according to the legends. Vampires slept beneath old churches in coffins or in mausoleums exactly like these. She heard Martin's hand slap against the cold stone.

'This here is my bed,' he said. Tess didn't hear him move, but a moment later his voice came from another part of the chamber, near where the rats were working.

'And this, if you agree, will be yours.'

Tess shuddered at the thought. 'No way.'

'No? Perhaps you'd better hear me out, first?'

'If you like. But nothing you can say is going to convince me.'

'Convince you of what?'

'Convince me to become a vampire.'

The voice was smooth as ever, and tinged with a touch of triumph. 'But I don't need to persuade you to become a vampire, Tess. You are one already.'

CHAPTER SIXTEEN

'Don't be ridiculous,' said Tess, aware that she was speaking into a darkness that was impenetrable to her eyes. 'I'm not.'

'Don't believe me, eh? You really haven't done your homework, have you?'

'Perhaps I have, perhaps I haven't. But I know one thing for certain, and that is I'm not going to discuss anything down here in this dungeon. There's no air. I can't breathe properly.'

Martin considered for a moment, then said, 'Fair enough, I suppose. I need to take a look at the surface anyway.'

There were various exit tunnels, but Martin, in rat form, led Tess up the least arduous of them. On the surface they found themselves among trees and, after a careful check around, they Switched back to the way they had been beneath ground.

The place they were in seemed familiar. Tess knew

the park well, but it was a good while before she got her bearings and realised that they were very close to the place where she and her parents had been playing frisbee earlier that day. The dip in the ground where they stood made sense now that she knew there was a cavern beneath and that the roof had begun to subside, but there was no sign at all of any church. If there had been one, it must have been destroyed or abandoned and the stones cleared away to be used in other buildings.

She glanced across at Martin, hoping he had chosen to be human for this encounter, but there was no such luck. The pallor of his cheeks and the shape of his mouth made it clear what he was, even in the darkness. Even so, she was glad to be out in the open where she would have more chance of escape.

'All right, then,' she said, 'let's hear what you have to say.'

The vampire began to approach, but Tess held out a hand like a traffic policeman. 'Stay where you are. I can hear you perfectly well from there.'

He laughed. 'If it makes you feel better. But you don't need to worry. I've already fed tonight.'

The trees rustled in the wind. The clear weather of the previous days had given way to heavy cloud rolling in from the west. Tess had no coat and she had left her hair-band on top of the piano at home, so her hair was blowing around all over the place. They were small worries, though, compared with what she was confronting.

'Well?' she said. 'Explain to me just how it is that you think I'm a vampire.'

'I don't think. I know. Have you forgotten what happened that night in Dorset Street?'

'Nothing happened. I Switched, that's all.'

'You Switched all right. But you were too slow. Don't you remember my teeth on your throat?'

Tess remembered all too well: the icy pinpricks, the feeling of being sucked under.

'It took you too long to make up your mind,' Martin was saying. 'I tasted your blood. I made you mine.'

Tess's jaw stiffened. There was steel in her veins. 'What do you mean, "yours"?'

'You really don't know, do you? I thought you were just acting stupid, but it's true, isn't it? You really haven't read the stories.'

Tess scowled at him, aware that her position was growing weaker by the minute. Martin hissed at her, 'Everyone whom the undead feed upon become theirs, didn't you realise? Oh, you'll go on living, all right. You might even lead a normal enough life, provided you can stay out of my way when I'm hungry. It's not the same for you, of course, but most people never even know that they have been my victims. Until they die, that is. Then they know. As you will know, when you become like me. One of the undead, one of my minions, until the end of time.'

Tess was silent, absorbing the horror of what he had said. That fact wasn't new to her, after all, even though she hadn't remembered it. It was basic to the myth; the main reason that was always given for the need to wipe out vampires.

'Your phoenix,' Martin went on, 'is doing a great job in spreading his sweetness and light, but do you think it will last? Do you think people will go on dancing on the grass and being delighted with each other? Give them a few days and they'll forget it all, go back to their drab and selfish little existences as if nothing had ever happened. But in the meantime I'll be going from strength to strength. Some of the older people I've preyed on will be joining me quite soon, and then they'll start recruiting for themselves. So in fifty years' time I'll have an army of followers, and every one of them a vampire, practically impossible to defeat. You should be thankful to me, Tess. I've made you immortal!'

The word caused a freezing tide to race up Tess's spine. To be immortal, to live for ever, that was what all this was about. The trees huffed again and Tess looked up at them. They were so strong and serene, so much of this world, the here and now. For the moment she needed to be like them, living in the present and not in the world of future possibilities. It comforted her to see herself not as she might be but as she was: a schoolgirl, about to enter her Junior Cert year. The trees moved in the breeze. The winter grass lay tangled at her feet.

'This is ridiculous!' she shouted. 'I'm not immortal and nor are you. You're just a boy, Martin, however you've dressed yourself up with your special power! Tomorrow you'll be lying in your bed watching a video!'

Her voice was high and full of emotion but his, when he replied, was as deep and calm as a bogland lake.

'I won't, though. That's why I called you here tonight.' Despite the darkness and the distance between them, Tess could make out the cruel smile of satisfaction on his face as he went on, 'I'm glad you told me about that fifteenth birthday stuff. I might have been caught on the hop if you hadn't. It's tomorrow, you see. My fifteenth birthday.'

He waited, watching her reaction as she struggled against a fate which seemed to be blocking her at every turn. When she made no answer, he continued, 'I want you to be with me, Tess. I'm going to be the master of this city and you can rule it by my side, but only if you come with me now; share my hideout down below. No one will ever find us there. We'll be safe. We'll be able to come and go as we please.'

His voice was persuasive, reaching beyond her defences to the part of her mind that was vampire. She found herself wondering why she was bothering to put up such a resistance. What was so wonderful about her life, after all? She existed in a state of almost total isolation; there was no one she could share her secrets with apart from Martin, and even he would be gone soon. It was clear now that she wasn't going to have any more adventures like the one which had taken her and Kevin across the planet in search of the krools, and even if she did, no one would ever know about her powers. She still felt resentful when she saw members of the US armed forces taking credit for ending the climatic threat, when it had been she and Kevin who had done it. She missed him, as well, even after all this time. She had been so delighted to see him return as a phoenix, but what good had it done her? She was as lonely as ever, and he was locked up in the zoo. It seemed to make so much sense, here in the darkness, just to let go of all resistance and slide along with the current. No one would ever tell her what to do again. The world would be hers for the taking.

But it would be a world of perpetual night. She would never see daylight again.

'No!' she said, surprised by her own decisiveness. 'I'll never agree to it.'

Martin shrugged, calm as ever. 'Suit yourself. You're mine anyway. But if you don't come now, if you wait for your death instead, you'll be nothing special to me then. You'll just be one among millions, serving me, spreading my power. It's up to you.'

'Yes. It is up to me,' said Tess, her voice strangely different, as calm now as his was. Because as he was speaking, the conflict of the last few days had suddenly become sparklingly clear in her mind. There wasn't just one kind of immortality being presented to her; there were two.

'But what if I don't die?' she went on. 'Then what will you do?'

'What do you mean, if you don't die? Everyone dies.'

'What if I became a phoenix instead? What would happen then?'

Now it was Martin's turn to be stunned into silence. For a long time the two of them stood facing one another while the trees leant over them, nodding in the breeze as though discussing the possible outcome. Then the vampire straightened up and moved a single step forward.

'If I hadn't already gorged myself tonight I would settle the issue here and now. But it doesn't matter. Your dayglo friend won't win out. How long do you think he can go on burning away like that before his gas runs out?'

'I don't know. What difference does it make, anyway? He'll rise up again, whenever he needs to.'

'You think so? What if there aren't any ashes for him to rise out of, eh? Does anyone know what happens then?'

'Ashes are only metaphorical. He'll rise again no matter what the circumstances are.'

'How do you know? Has it ever been tested?'

'You don't need to test things like that. You just know them.'

'Do you?' As he spoke, the vampire seemed to be swelling and moving towards her, like a shadow with a light receding behind it. 'Well, I don't.'

A black cloud passed over Tess's head and vanished into the night. She stood still for a moment, searching the empty skies. Then something began to tug at the edge of her mind. Something urgent and demanding, making her restless and fidgety. Something she was supposed to do? Something she'd forgotten? She let down her guard and the message flooded in. It was being sent in Rat, and to her rat mind it was utterly irresistible.

'Top speed to the zoo. Phoenix is the enemy. Tear it to pieces.'

Tess took a few strides in the direction of the zoo, but realised that it was useless to try and go above ground. Now she knew why the dirt floor and gravel in the exhibition building had seemed so important to her that day.

That was the only way in.

CHAPTER SEVENTEEN

Tess Switched and made a dive for the nearest tunnel. Despite the huge underground mesh of interlinking passages, she had no problem finding the quickest route to the zoo. Rats work according to a precise logic of their own, and although it would have made no sense to her human mind, the way was clear and simple.

By the time she reached the well-established network of runs beneath the zoo, the place was stiff with rats. They had come from all corners of the city, some above ground but most of them below, and they were still pouring in. Despite the apparent chaos, work was already proceeding in an orderly manner. Tess asked around and soon got the low-down on what was happening. New tunnels were being constructed beneath the exhibition building and back-up parties were ferrying the freshly-dug soil and rubble out to the surface, emerging among the bushes and spreading the debris around carefully to avoid detection.

Tess joined one of the earth-shifting teams. She made sure that she pulled her weight and did nothing to delay the proceedings, but whenever she got the opportunity she dodged forward a place in the line, working her way towards the head of the tunnelling team.

She had no idea what she was going to do. Her human mind was struggling desperately to rise above the instinctual mire of rat behaviour, but it was about as successful as a moth in a jar of honey. Occasional insight broke clear, but it was always the same: she had made an awful mistake, betrayed Kevin, and there was nothing she could do to stop the impending horror.

As she worked, still edging her way closer to the lead diggers, she kept a close eye open for any rats that she knew. If she could find Algernon, or Nose Broken by a Mousetrap – even stupid old Long Nose – she might be able to win them over. Between them they might spread the word and talk some sense into the rest of the rats. But she had about as much chance of meeting them as of meeting a long-lost friend in a football crowd. There were hundreds of rats working on her particular tunnel, but not one of them was known to her. With an increasing sense of dread, she worked on.

There seemed to be nothing else to do. Even if she deserted the rat legions and went out on to the surface she would still be helpless. She had long since ruled out the possibility of releasing the phoenix on her own, since there was no way of getting into the exhibition hall apart from this underground route. The only thing she could do was to be there when the final confrontation happened, and to pray that the vampire was wrong about the weakness of the phoenix power. She could hardly stand to think about what would happen if he wasn't.

The going became more difficult as the tunnellers began to bore into the heavy rubble foundations of the building. Reports were coming in from various separate reconnaissance teams. There were two men in the building, apparently, keeping watch on the phoenix. Of the several dozen tunnels that were under construction, eight of them were on target, right beneath the phoenix's cage.

The rats abandoned the useless tunnels and gathered where they would be ready to pour into the good ones as they were completed. The ground beneath the glass cage babbled with images as the rats reported their progress to each other, their vivid communications passing easily through mud, stone or concrete. But above their heads, where Jeff Maloney sat playing cards with a highly-paid guard from a security company, there was no way of knowing that anything was going on.

Extra workers were drafted in to dig holes in the tunnel walls so that large stones being moved out of the foundations could be lodged instead of being dragged all the way out. The lead tunnellers, Tess among them, wove their way around the biggest stones, loosening the smaller rubble and shoving it back to the next in line. Then, suddenly, the leading rat froze as a tiny shower of loose sand and earth dropped down on to her nose.

Jeff Maloney turned his head at the sound of a few white quartz pebbles moving in the phoenix's cage. The lights were turned off so that the bird could sleep, and the only illumination in the building came from a small lamp on the table where the two men were playing their game. The phoenix was on its perch, high above the potted shrubs, sleeping soundly. Only the dimmest radiance gleamed from its feathers.

'Probably a mouse,' said Jeff.

'What was?'

'That noise. Didn't you hear it?'

The security guard shook his head. 'You keep mice as well?'

'They keep themselves. And rats. The animal food attracts them, and all the rubbish the visitors leave. Nothing you can do about them.'

There was a dozy pause, then Jeff said, 'Whose go is it?'

Beneath their feet, Tess and her team were waiting for the other tunnels to be ready. To be sure of working, the attack had to be coordinated properly. A constant stream of visual messages passed between the members of the rodent army. They were almost ready.

Jeff and the guard swung round, instantly alert, as a half-dozen holes opened in the ground beneath the phoenix and pebbles began to pour into them. Jeff leapt to his feet and jumped for the main light switch. Cards fluttered across empty space as the guard threw down his hand and grabbed for the pistol he carried beneath his jacket.

Then the floor of the cage disappeared as a flood of rats welled up like a spring from below. Before Jeff could disentangle the key of the cage from the handkerchief in his pocket, the rats had streamed up the foliage and were beginning to take leaps at the perch where the phoenix still sat. In the nick of time he spread his wings, rose into the air and hovered there, just below the ceiling.

'Get help!' yelled Jeff.

The security guard, who had become glued to the floor at the sight of so many rats, needed no second bidding to get out. He raced for the main door, threw the bolt, and disappeared into the darkness outside.

Against the glass wall of the cage, Tess sat and watched as Jeff Maloney unlocked the door and slid it open. He was the one who had caught the magnificent bird, and despite his horror of the swarming rats, he had no hesitation in going to its rescue. He strode into the cage, oblivious to the outraged squeaks of the rats beneath his feet and, kicking clear a space for himself, stood on the edge of the tallest plant pot. From there he took a lunge at the perch, making it swing so violently that it dislodged the rats who were squirrelling up its suspension chains in their efforts to get at the floating phoenix.

The bird was still too high for Jeff to reach. With a Tarzan-like leap, he grabbed the perch and swung himself up, grabbing the phoenix by its three-toed foot before the chain links snapped and he dropped back to his feet on the carpet of rats, breaking several backbones.

Tess pushed her way through the throng as Jeff leapt out of the cage and raced across the building. She was at his heels, but others were there before her, climbing up his clothes, swarming all over his body and up the arm he was holding above his head with the phoenix at the end of it.

The bird flapped desperately as the rats reached it and the first set of teeth sank into its leg. Jeff struck out frantically with his free hand, but he was losing the battle. He was up to his knees in rats, wading through a sea of them, and as quickly as he could knock them from his clothes and face, they were being replaced by others.

Outside, the security man had failed to find help and was running back towards the building. He arrived just in time to see Jeff give in and let go of the phoenix in a desperate attempt to save himself. Through a gap in the clawing and clambering madness, Tess saw the phoenix dart out through the open door and soar away above the zoo.

Both Jeff and the guard were far too busy with the rats to notice a small, dark bird emerging from their midst and setting off in pursuit of the phoenix. They were thrashing and kicking around them like a pair of windmills. But to their surprise, as soon as the phoenix was out of sight, the rats did a complete about-face and vanished back into the ground, leaving the dead and the dying behind.

CHAPTER EIGHTEEN

The phoenix swept up and out over the park, each beat of its small wings giving it height, so that it appeared to move in a series of great bounds. Tess's swallow wings worked at double speed as she tried to keep up. The easiest way would have been to become a phoenix herself, but the human part of her mind could see that would be a foolish move. The other bird had become dim enough by now to be difficult to see, even above the relative darkness of the park, but Tess assumed that if she became a phoenix she would be as bright as ever and would draw attention just when they needed to shake it off.

The phoenix took another upward leap and the swallow flapped after it. A few minutes more would be enough. They were almost over the middle of the park now, and would soon be too high for anyone to see. Then Tess could Switch into phoenix form and become comfortable. After that, once they were safely clear of the city, they could rest and decide what the future might be.

Once more the phoenix leapt skyward. Once more, Tess drove her small wings to the limit. It was enough, surely. Below them, the park was a black island of emptiness in the middle of a lake of orange light. Even if someone down there did spot her now, they were surely beyond any danger.

But even as she prepared for the Switch, visualising the form she was about to take and remembering how it felt, a dark shape appeared out of nowhere and collided with the phoenix, knocking it off balance and sending it tumbling down towards the earth.

Tess closed her wings and dropped like a stone. Beneath her, the phoenix flapped and turned in the air, slowing its descent and finally recovering control. It began to climb again and Tess swooped beneath it, struggling to stay close. Out of the darkness the shadow reappeared and this time Tess could see that it was a huge bat, its wings stretched taut as it glided with deadly accuracy straight into the phoenix.

Again the phoenix fell, righted itself, began to ascend. Again the huge bat took aim and slammed into it. Tess fluttered wildly, first up and then down, her only objective being to stay as close to the phoenix as she could.

The battle was hopeless. Each time the bat hit the phoenix, the bird lost more height and, Tess thought, as it got closer to the trees below, it seemed to lose heart as well. Eventually it gave up and spread its wings to glide down between the branches and come to rest, sitting on the air a few feet above the ground.

Tess plunged after the phoenix, banking and twisting through the trees. Even before she had quite landed, she Switched back into human form, desperate for the full use of her human mind to work out what was going on. She stumbled as she landed, and found herself face down in the cool, damp grass. The wind was still waffling round in the trees and for a long moment Tess lay still where she had fallen, breathing in the damp scent of the earth and wishing she could stay there for ever. But out of the corner of her eye, she caught a glimpse of movement as the dark shape of the bat flitted into the copse, its leathery wings purring through the air. As it landed, it seemed to expand, and by the time Tess stood up it was the vampire that stood there, pale face set into a grin of satisfaction.

'He's a pushover,' he said.

'No!' Tess found herself standing between the two adversaries, just a few feet from each of them. The phoenix made no further attempt to escape, but hung in the air, his feathers casting a pale glow over the group.

'No?' said the vampire. 'But why not? You were so certain that Humpty Dumpty could put himself back together again. Are you not so sure now?'

'Of course I am! That's not the point.'

'What is the point then, Tess?'

The voice was soft as sleep, reaching out to her, drawing her in. With a tremendous effort of will she wrenched her attention away from it and fixed her eyes on the phoenix. It was still floating above the ground, unaffected by the strengthening gusts of wind that blew through the copse. Its eyes were on a level with hers, its gaze steady and fearless.

'Which way, Tess?'

Her eyelids drooped. Her gaze lost its focus, then shifted back to rest upon the vampire as he spoke.

'You have to make up your mind, you know. Come with me willingly and I'll leave your friend alone to go back to the chicken coop. How's that for a deal?'

It seemed reasonable, especially when she looked into the deep, soulless eyes and remembered the night they had hunted together, the entire city theirs for the taking. She was tired of struggling for what seemed to be right all the time. There was no reward for that, in the end. She had lost her best friend, and the creature that hung in the air beside her wasn't him, even if it once had been. Why shouldn't she become a vampire? What was the point of resisting? But as she began to turn, her attention drifting towards that dark, eternal power, the phoenix seemed to brighten for a moment, and the glow which emanated from him was reflected in the vampire's eyes, which glowed like a cat's in a car's headlights. The connection broke. Tess gasped and turned back to the phoenix. It continued to hang on the air, silent and motionless. As Tess opened herself to its influence again she began to feel warmth and life flowing through her, as though some lost flame had been rekindled within. Without knowing why she did it, she lifted her right arm and stretched out her hand towards the phoenix.

'No, Tess,' came the rich, silky voice of the vampire. 'Think again. Is that really what you want? All that twinkle, twinkle, little star stuff? Come with me, come on. Before it's too late.'

He was holding out his hand. All she had to do was take it. Her left hand reached out.

The wind came straight at her like a slap in the face, sobering her, bringing her, for a moment, back to reality. She was standing in the woods like a scarecrow, one hand stretching towards a golden light, the other towards perpetual darkness. It was like a crazy dream, where the only thing that was real was the wind in her face, carrying the fresh flavours of all the places it had been, reminding her how alive she was right now.

To either side, eternities were pulling at her and she was stretched between them, standing on a razor's edge. She needed help, and cast around for some of those words of wisdom she was forever being crammed with in her religion classes. But the only words that came to her were Lizzie's.

'Trust yourself, girl. You'll know what to do when the time comes.'

'But I don't!' she yelled at her mind's image of the old woman. The two forces were working against each other now, so powerfully that Tess could no longer tell whether she were being torn apart or crushed between them. The dark shadow of the vampire was expanding, looming above her. On the other side, the phoenix was brightening, its light growing all around it until the two seemed about to meet over her head. And at that moment, Tess felt her left hand grasp the vampire's fingers and her right catch hold of the phoenix's three-toed foot.

A charge like an electric current went through her body and numbed her brain as the two forces met within her, on equal terms now, and began to do battle. Wild fantasies played through her mind as the protagonists took shapes for themselves, using the raw material of Tess's imagination. Angels and demons fought there, armies of light and dark, red and blue, good and evil. Characters came forward and spoke to her, each taking one side or the other, each as persuasive as the one before.

In the midst of it all, Tess swung from one allegiance to the other. One moment she was certain that the phoenix was the better choice and the next there seemed no doubt that the vampire was. What was it Lizzie had said about choice? 'It's not always what we are that needs changing, but the way we thinks.' What was that supposed to mean? How on earth could it help her?

The struggle worsened. The opponents seemed to be tearing at her sense of herself, destroying her confidence. If she did not choose soon, one way or the other, she would surely be damaged by the conflict. But what could she do? What was wrong with the way she was thinking?

As if in reply, one strong, clear thought began to emerge. Throughout the whole of the struggle she had not once had the impression that either the vampire or phoenix cared about her; about Tess, the individual. All either of them wanted was to attain superiority, even if she was sacrificed in the process. Suddenly she knew what Lizzie meant. Tess was burdened by choice only because she felt that she must choose one or the other. But the truth was that she didn't have to be either. If she could just rise out of this turmoil and feel the wind on her face once again, it would be worth all the fears and the pains and the longings of being merely mortal.

A new determination entered Tess's heart. She was part of the light and the dark and their struggle, but they were a part of her, too. She would not be vampire and she would not be phoenix. Later, if and when life made sense again, she would worry about her fifteenth birthday. But for the moment she could only deal with the present. She took a deep breath and, with a mighty effort, she gathered all her forces together and broke free of the grips on her hands.

'I just want to be human!' she yelled.

Jeff Maloney heard that extraordinary shout as he plunged into the copse where he was sure he had seen his precious bird descending. What he saw was totally unexpected. There were three teenagers in there on the grass: two boys and a girl, all of them strewn around the glade as though they had just been dropped from a height. For a moment Jeff was so surprised by the sight that he forgot what he was looking for.

'Hello?' he said, shining his torch on them, one after another. The girl looked exhausted, as though she had just survived some horrendous ordeal, and Jeff might have suspected the boys of some savagery towards her if they had not looked as dazed as she did. One of them, a mousy-looking fellow, was looking around him as though he was seeing the planet for the first time. The other, red-headed, was as white as a sheet, like someone who has just been in an accident.

'What's going on?'

Tess screwed up her eyes against the flashlight. 'Who's there? she said. Beside her, Kevin was shielding his eyes with his arm and looking over at Martin, who had buried his face in his hands. They looked odd, all three of them, but Jeff could see that they were all right, and his mind went back to his search. He turned his flashlight off and looked up into the trees.

'Anyone seen a bird come to land here? A golden one?'

The girl and one of the boys shook their heads

solemnly. The other boy seemed not to hear, but let out a sudden shout. 'Dad! I'm sorry, Dad. I didn't mean it!'

Tess struggled to her feet and went over to Martin. He was crying now, his whole body shuddering.

'I didn't mean it,' he gasped between sobs. 'I was going to go for help but I couldn't. The cow was in the road, heaving about the place. The stupid cow!'

Tess rested a hand on Martin's shoulder, frustrated by her helplessness in the face of his pain.

'I didn't mean to kill him, Tess.'

'You didn't kill him. It was an accident.'

'I did. I did kill him. I wished he was dead and he died. I killed him.'

He broke down again and Tess fell silent, knowing that words were useless.

Jeff Maloney was glued to the spot, torn between concern for the boy's distress and the urgent desire to search for his bird.

'Has there been some sort of an accident?' he said to Tess, quietly. She shook her head.

As Jeff lingered, still unsure what to do, two of his colleagues from the zoo ran up. They had been following the light of his torch for some time. Their arrival solved his dilemma.

'The bird is around here somewhere,' he said. 'I saw it come down. Will you keep on searching?' He nodded towards Martin and Tess. 'I'm not sure what's going on here, but I want to get this lot home.'

The others agreed and Jeff approached the huddled figures on the ground. His voice was friendly and reassuring.

'You're all right now. Tell me where you live and I'll drive you home. My car's parked on the road just back there.'

As Jeff spoke, Martin became silent and tense beneath Tess's hand. It was one thing to reveal his pain to her, but quite another to be caught, vulnerable, in front of a stranger. Before Tess knew what was happening he was on his feet.

'Leave me alone,' he yelled at Jeff. Then he raced away between the trees.

Tess set off in pursuit. There was barely light to see by, but she could just make out Martin's slight figure weaving through the tree trunks. He was fast, but as Tess ran after him she knew that she was, too. It was as though the resolution of that dreadful conflict had made energy available to her that she hadn't known she possessed. And every ounce of it had to be used in making sure she didn't lose her friend in the darkness. Because he was a friend, now. She had held her own ground, pulled the opposing forces together instead of allowing them to pull her apart, and in doing so she had not only made herself whole, but the others as well. Kevin, she knew, could look after himself, but she wasn't so sure about Martin; not now that his defences were down and he was exposed to all that old pain. He had closed off his feelings when his father was killed, safe within the vampire's cold shell. But now he would have to experience all that shock and fear and sorrow as though the accident had just happened. He was in danger, not only from the stress itself but from the possibility of reverting to the familiar protection of the vampire existence. It was vital that Tess should stay with him.

Ahead of her, he dodged left and right around a tree stump, heading for open ground. With renewed confidence, Tess made straight for the stump, certain that she could jump it and gain ground. She timed her run perfectly and jumped well clear of the decaying wood, but as she landed, her feet went from under her and she came down hard, flat on her back.

The wind was knocked right out of her and for a few moments she found herself gazing at the blank face of the starless sky, wondering if her end had come. Then, just as it seemed she could hold on no longer, her chest relaxed and she pulled in a long, cool breath.

'Are you all right?' It was Kevin, leaning over her, his face filled with concern. He must have been right behind her. She tried to smile but there were more urgent priorities and for another minute she had to gasp for air, until her breath caught up with itself.

Kevin looked out across the park, but it was already too late. By the time Tess recovered sufficiently to sit up, Martin was long gone into the darkness.

'I landed on something,' said Tess, still panting. 'It slid along the ground and I skidded.'

Kevin kicked around in the grass, then bent and picked something up: a flat disc the size of a dinner plate. Tess reached out and took it from him.

'My frisbee!' she said. 'My useless, flaming frisbee.'

CHAPTER NINETEEN

It was ten past eleven, according to Tess's wristwatch, and the first rain was just starting to dampen the breeze. Kevin reached out a hand and helped Tess to her feet. It was the first chance she'd had to get a good look at him and she found herself grinning with delight.

'You haven't changed a bit,' she said, tugging at the lapel of his faded khaki jacket.

'Not on the outside, maybe,' he said, tossing back his long, wispy fringe with a familiar shake of the head. 'But I've changed an awful lot on the inside.'

He looked around him and, from the expression of wonderment on his face, he might have been standing at the foot of the Himalayas. 'I never thought it could happen. I wanted it to . . . you've no idea . . . but I never dreamt it could.'

'It probably wouldn't if it hadn't been for Martin.'

'I suppose so. There had to be an opposite. But if it hadn't been for you . . .'

Tess shuddered, remembering more than she wanted to about the battle that had been waged inside her mind. Whatever else might happen to her in life, she didn't want to go through that again.

'We shouldn't stand around, though,' she said. 'It mightn't be over yet.'

'What do you mean?'

'It's Martin's fifteenth birthday tomorrow. There's no guaranteeing that he'll stay the way he is now. It might all be too much for him; he might decide to become a vampire in spite of everything that's happened. And if he does . . .'

'If he does, what?'

'Come on. I'll tell you as we go.'

Tess looked around to get her bearings, then they set off, walking as fast as they could in the direction of Phibsboro. Here and there, torches flashed among the trees and desolate voices drifted on the wind as the zoo staff continued to hunt for the phoenix.

'Tough on them,' said Tess, but Kevin just laughed until he choked. By the time he had recovered his composure they had reached the city streets and, as they walked along, Tess told the whole story and explained about the vampire's method of spreading its influence.

'So you see,' she concluded, 'if he does become a vampire, then I will, too, when I'm dead.'

'You could still opt for the phoenix.'

'I might, if it came with recommendations. But you don't seem to have any regrets about being human again.'

'No, I don't,' said Kevin. 'The phoenix was glorious. I don't have to tell you – you know how it feels.

153

But it was too .. I don't know how to describe it. Too perfect, or too high and mighty or something. Too lonely.'

There was an awkward silence as they both became aware of the personal meaning in his words. Kevin coloured with embarrassment, but made no attempt to retract what he had said. They had missed each other more than either of them cared to admit, yet neither was prepared to reveal their fondness. In the end, Kevin changed the subject.

'So, if he does go vampire, we'll only have one option, won't we?'

That word 'we' was one of the finest sounds that Tess had ever heard. She realised how lonely she, too, had been over the past months.

'What's that?' she said.

'Well. You know where he'll be sleeping during the day, don't you? We'll just have to dig our way in there and do the old stake through the heart job.'

He spoke as if it were an everyday occurrence, like swatting a wasp with a newspaper. But the prospect filled Tess with horror.

'I hope we find him first,' she said. 'I prefer diplomatic solutions on the whole.'

It was nearly midnight when they reached Martin's house in Phibsboro. There were no lights on, but Tess took a chance and knocked on the door. As they waited, the rain worsened and blew against them, soaking into their hair and dripping down their necks. Tess wriggled with discomfort but Kevin didn't seem to notice, partly because he was still overawed at being human again. He gazed round at the dull houses as though he was in Disneyland. Tess sighed and knocked again.

'It's no good,' she said. 'If he's in, he's not answering. Wait here, will you?'

She was on the point of Switching into a rat when she remembered the compelling power that the vampire still held over all the rats' minds in the city. On impulse she tried a mouse instead, and found immediate entry into the house by way of a missing chip of concrete underneath the front door.

The hall was vast to her tiny eyes, stretching upwards and outwards into a dark oblivion. It was full of smells, alive with them; some appealing, others threatening. Mouse life was about weighing up the balance of the scents in the air all around. If danger weighed too heavily, then a change of plan was required. If it didn't, a chance was worth taking. But at that moment, it was all too much for Tess's already exhausted mind, so she Switched into a cat instead and padded swiftly and silently up the carpeted staircase. Outside Martin's room she Switched back to human shape again and, with her heart in her mouth, pushed open the door.

Inside it was too dark to see anything. The video clock, still mindlessly flashing, distracted her attention and left dizzying green patches on her retinas. She held out a hand to block it from view.

'Martin?'

If he had got home, he couldn't have been there for long; certainly not long enough to get to sleep. She listened carefully, but there was no sound of breathing. Her skin crawled as she suddenly imagined the vampire there beside her, leaning across in the darkness . . .

With a hand that trembled slightly, she felt around behind the door frame until she found the light switch and flicked it down. The bare bulb blinded her for a moment, but even as she squinted and blinked she could see that the room was empty. The bedclothes were crumpled and the floor beside the bed was cluttered with the familiar collection of socks and tea cups and video cases. Everything was as usual, except for Martin. Tess swore to herself in a whisper. Because if he wasn't there, where was he?

She turned out the light, became a cat again, and was just about to go back down the stairs when her sharp eyes noticed another door along the landing which stood ajar. The black hair along her spine stood up as she remembered Martin's anaemic mother. If he was taking a late-night snack she would rather not know about it. But she had to. If there was any chance at all of getting to him before dawn, she had to take it.

Martin's mother was alone in the room, sleeping on her back in a battered old double bed that she must once have shared with her husband. Her face was deathly white in the dim light which entered from the street and for a moment Tess feared the worst. But as she slipped across the floor, her paws making no sound on the nylon carpet, Tess's sensitive ears picked up the faint rise and fall of shallow breath. She was alive, but undoubtedly weak. The implications were obvious. If Martin remained human, she would recover; her anaemia passing away as mysteriously as it had come. But if he chose to live out his existence as a vampire, then one more feed could finish her off and she would become like him: the first of many.

Would she take that other stone coffin, the one that Martin had reserved for Tess? Would Tess and Kevin have to bring two stakes down into the crypt with them, to be sure of finishing the job?

The black cat turned and bounded down the stairs, becoming a mouse between the bottom step and the floor and tumbling along the ground a few times as it slowed down. It flowed like toothpaste under the door and disappeared beneath the foot of a girl who hadn't been there a moment before. Luckily there was no one there to see the first part, and the only person who saw the girl appear was not surprised at all.

'Well?' he said.

'Not there.'

He sighed. 'Looks bad, doesn't it?'

'Maybe. Maybe he just needs time on his own to try and come to terms with things.'

Kevin looked around as though he hoped to see beyond the buildings into the darkness. Out there somewhere was either a boy coping with a private grief or a being on the point of entering perpetual night.

Tess shivered. Kevin slipped out of his parka and hung it over her bony shoulders.

'Your turn,' he said, before she could object.

It was heavy with rain, but still warm. Tess glanced up and down the street, hoping against hope to see Martin strolling down the pavement towards them. But from one end of the street to the other, nothing moved.

'I suppose there's no point in standing here,' she said. 'We might as well go home.'

CHAPTER TWENTY

It was well into the early hours of the morning by the time Tess and Kevin got home to her house on the edge of the park. Kevin shivered as he waited for Tess to turn the key in the lock. She looked at him and shrugged, abandoning them both to whatever trouble lay in store for them, then pushed the door open.

Immediately there was a noise from the direction of the living room: the flutter and slap of a newspaper being hastily thrown aside. A moment later Tess's father appeared in the hall, his face taut with worry which was rapidly turning to anger. He stopped dead in the middle of the hallway when he saw Tess's companion and an awkward silence hung on the air as she closed the front door behind them and slipped out of Kevin's jacket.

'Dad, this is a friend of mine, Kevin.'

Her father nodded, wrong-footed, uncertain

whether the occasion called for civility or righteous indignation. Before he could make up his mind, his wife appeared at the head of the stairs in her dressing-gown.

'Oh, there you are, Tess. Where on earth have you been?'

Tess hung the sodden jacket on a spare hook inside the door. 'It's a long story, I'm afraid.'

'You're not getting out of it that easy,' said her father. 'I don't care how long the story is, I want to hear it.'

Tess's mind threatened to go on strike. The best she could dredge up was the same excuse she had given them in the park earlier that day.

'We had to go and call on that sick friend. The one I was telling you about.'

'Oh, I see.' Her father's tone betrayed his scepticism. 'The sick friend again. And you were there until one-thirty in the morning, were you?'

'Not exactly. But we ran into a few difficulties.'

'Clearly. And for some reason you decided to bring one of them home with you.'

'Seamus!' said Tess's mother reproachfully. 'Don't talk about Tess's friends like that. Not without giving them a chance, at least.'

'Right,' said Tess, looking cryptically at Kevin. She needed help, but from the look of him she was unlikely to get it. He was standing with his hands in his pockets, dripping on to the hall carpet and looking self-conscious. Tess felt sure he was going to get sulky and clam up, the way he had with Lizzie, but to her surprise he pushed his wet hair out of his eyes and said, 'The phoenix escaped from the zoo. We met the zoo-keepers searching for it.'

'Yes,' said Tess. 'I saw it escape and I followed it.'

'Then she slipped on a frisbee and knocked the stuffing out of herself.'

'Oh, Tess. Did you?'

'Yes. But I'm OK, honestly. It just delayed us a bit. And now it's too late for Kevin to get home. So can he stay the night?'

Tess's father looked from one to the other, suspiciously.

'Is all this really true? It sounds very unlikely.'

'It's true. Every word of it,' said Tess.

'And what about your sick friend? Where does he fit in?'

Tess felt sick herself at being reminded of Martin. He could be out there in the night, feeding on some poor innocent's blood, preparing to return to his new underground bedroom. She glanced at Kevin as she said, 'We missed him in the end. We'll have to try again tomorrow.'

Tess's mother came down the stairs, the long hem of her dressing-gown covering her bare feet. She stood in front of Kevin and looked closely at him, as though trying to see into his soul. Then she said, 'Does your mother know where you are?'

'No,' said Kevin, looking her straight in the eye. 'But then, she never does. She doesn't take any interest, really. She certainly won't be worried about me.'

'Are you sure?'

'Positive.'

She examined him for a few seconds longer, then sighed. 'Well, whatever else you do, you'd better get out of those wet clothes before you catch pneumonia. Do either of you want a bath?'

Tess shook her head, but Kevin nodded eagerly.

'Yes, please. I can't remember the last time I had a bath!'

Tess cringed and her father looked astonished, but her mother laughed and gestured to Kevin to follow her up the stairs. She exchanged a complicitous smile with Tess over the bannisters which made her heart swell with pleasure. At least she had one ally in the house.

When she had towelled herself down and put on dry clothes, Tess sorted out a genderless tracksuit and left it outside the bathroom door. Then she went to help her mother, who was making up the bed in the spare room for Kevin.

'What about this sick friend of yours?' she said. 'You're being very mysterious about him.'

'Oh, there's nothing so mysterious, really.' As she spoke, Tess realised that despite their conspiratorial understanding of a few minutes before, they could never understand each other about some things. 'He's under a lot of stress,' she went on. 'His father died in an accident and he hasn't really got over the shock of it yet. He needs a lot of support.'

'You should have told me before,' said her mother. 'I'm all in favour of you being helpful like that. Perhaps I could help, too? Bake a cake or something? Would he like that?'

Tess fought back the deluge of ironic laughter that threatened to swamp her faculties. She pictured her mother walking into the vampire's lair, entirely unsuspecting, holding out a perfect specimen of her famous Lemon Drizzle.

'He might,' she said. 'We'll have to wait and see how things turn out.'

They finished making the bed, then her mother turned on the electric blanket and went back to her own room. On her way downstairs, Tess met her father coming up with two cups of cocoa.

'Oh, thanks, Dad.'

'For what? These are for your mother and I. It's late enough as it is, and I'm supposed to be at the office early in the morning.'

'Oh.'

'There's plenty of milk in the fridge if you and your boyfriend want to make some.'

'He's not my boyfriend!'

'Good.' Her father's face softened and he moved both slopping mugs into one hand and reached out with the other to muss up Tess's damp hair. 'But whoever he is, don't be staying up all night, you hear? I don't know about him, but you have to be on the school bus at half past eight.'

School past, school future; both of them seemed light years away. But she nodded at her father and made a show of looking at her watch.

'Don't worry, Dad. We won't be up much longer.'

'Goodnight, then.'

'Goodnight.'

Tess had made cocoa and a pile of sandwiches before Kevin eventually finished soaking in the bath and came down. He was a fresh, pink colour, and his hands and feet were wrinkled like prunes. Together they raided the cupboards for crisps, biscuits and fruit, then they brought the whole feast up to Tess's bedroom.

'You've redecorated,' said Kevin, looking around him.

'Last year.' Tess put down the tray and slotted an R.E.M. tape into the cassette deck. 'My dad wanted to cheer me up.'

'Cheer you up? Why?'

Tess blushed and turned away, not wanting to tell Kevin how upset she had been when she thought he was dead, and how strongly it had affected her life. The music began with a boom, and she grabbed for the volume control before it could wake her parents.

Kevin started into the sandwiches. Tess had made one with apricots and cashew nuts and put it on the top of the pile, and for a long time neither of them could do anything except laugh. When they finally recovered themselves, Kevin said, 'It's so good to be human again. You have no idea, Tess.'

'Really?' she said. 'I thought it was wonderful, being a phoenix.'

'It was, for a while. But it's like, what do you do once you're perfect? Nothing to be afraid of, nothing to strive for. Hardly living at all, really, is it?'

Tess shrugged. 'If you say so,' she said. 'But I'm still not sure how it happened, how you came to Switch back even though you're over fifteen.'

'I didn't get it to begin with, either, but I think I do, now. I think that I could only exist as a phoenix as long as Martin existed as a vampire. We counterbalanced each other in some way.'

'That's right,' said Tess. 'Lizzie said something like that. I just didn't understand it at the time.'

'And it was you who changed us, Tess. By deciding that you wouldn't become like either of us.'

'But how do you know I decided that?'

'I could feel it. I was part of the fight, remember?'

'Does that mean that Martin isn't a vampire, then?' said Tess.

'I don't know,' said Kevin. 'That would be the proof of the theory, I suppose, if it did. But I certainly wouldn't like to bank on it.'

They both fell silent, contemplating what he had said. Then Kevin said, 'Who lives in the cage?'

'No one.' Tess explained about Algernon and the vampire's control of the rats. As she spoke, they both became aware of the black, empty gaze of the window, and Kevin got up to draw the curtains.

'Do you think he's out there?' said Tess.

Kevin thought for a minute, and there was no sound apart from the tinny beat of music being played more quietly than it was meant to be.

'I don't know,' he said, 'but I feel as though I ought to. There should be some way of knowing, shouldn't there? Not logically, perhaps, but instinctively.'

Tess sat still, trying to work out what she felt. 'There's some kind of danger out there in the dark,' she said.

'I know that. But there always has been, hasn't there? And there always will be – places where it's not safe to be. Trouble is, it's like traffic accidents; you never know until it's too late.'

The mention of accidents reminded Tess of what she and Martin had been talking about. 'The crazy thing is, I don't blame him for what he did. I mean, shutting himself off like that and becoming cold and mean.'

Kevin surprised her. 'I do,' he said. 'It was his choice.'

The music played on, and it seemed like no time at all before the tape came to an end and Tess had to get up and turn it over. Kevin sat quietly in the chair, lost in his own thoughts. It didn't matter to Tess that he wasn't communicative; she didn't feel much like talking herself. It was enough that he was there.

The night slipped past. From time to time, Tess

thought about going to bed, but she knew that she wouldn't be able to sleep. Although neither of them said it, they were both waiting for the dawn and Tess noticed that, just as she did, Kevin regularly glanced up at the thin wedge or darkness where the curtains met.

Long before it began to get light, they heard Tess's father get up and go downstairs for breakfast. Soon afterwards he came up with tea for his wife. Tess waited for the regular knock on her door which woke her every morning, but it didn't come.

'He's letting me lie in,' she said quietly to Kevin.

'Lucky you.'

Tess laughed. 'I'm still not tired. But I keep telling myself how ridiculous it is to be sitting up like this.'

Kevin nodded, then looked again towards the window. Tess followed his eyes. The first hint of blue had crept into the blackness. She got up and drew the curtains, then switched off the light. When their eyes adjusted, they realised that there was more light in the day than they had thought.

'Is this dawn?' said Kevin. 'Does it count?'

'What difference does it make?' said Tess. 'We've no way of knowing what has happened, in any case.'

'I suppose not.'

'What are we going to do?'

'I don't know. Go looking, I suppose. With a good sharp stake of course.'

Tess shuddered, then sighed. 'I can't sleep. I just wish we had some way of knowing.'

As if in answer, there was a scuffle of tough little claws beneath the floorboards. Kevin froze, remembering the terrible attack the rats had made upon him when he was a phoenix. Was the vampire around, somewhere? Had he been hovering around all night, listening to them, and sent the rats to finish off Kevin before he could carry out his threat?

He stood up and looked around, horribly aware of his helplessness now that he no longer had the power to Switch. If the rats came for him here, there would be no way that he could escape.

Tess glanced over at him, understanding the situation immediately. Her mind went into overdrive as she searched for a solution. A terrier, perhaps? At least she could hold them at bay for a while.

But the nose that came poking through the gap in the wardrobe doors was very far from being aggressive. It was pink with white whiskers and it was twitching nervously. A white snout followed and a pair of weak, red eyes which peered anxiously around the room.

'Algernon!' said Tess.

The white rat heard her and moved cautiously into the room, sniffing the air and examining every object he encountered with grave suspicion. His nose was bumpy with scars and bruises, and his paws were swollen from digging.

'Poor Algie.' Tess bent down as he reached her foot, and stretched out a hand towards him. She was wary, remembering the fierce bite he had given her in the crypt, but this time there was no need to worry. Algernon jumped slightly as her fingers touched his grubby coat, then turned his head to sniff at her. Before she could get a hand around him, he ran up her sleeve and perched himself on her shoulder, pushing his twitching nose into the nape of her neck and up over her face.

'Apple, huh?' he said to her. 'White rat eating. White rat sleeping curled up in bed. Lots of shredded paper. Warm and cosy.'

Tess laughed in delight. 'White rat tired of tunnels and drains, huh?'

'White rat sleeping in cage. White rat running round on wheel.'

Kevin had been listening and now he bit a chunk out of an apple and handed it to Algernon, who sat up on Tess's shoulder and took it in his front paws. Eating didn't stop him from talking at all, since he didn't need his mouth to do it.

'Rat-bat-wolf-boy disappeared. Brown rats falling asleep on their feet. Sleeping in drains and tunnels. Whole city silent.'

Tess and Kevin said nothing, each of them dwelling on their own thoughts. Algernon finished the piece of apple and scuttled from Tess's shoulder into his cage. Tess was aware of a great sense of contentment. Lizzie had been right again and had helped her to do the right thing. Kevin was back, her parents seemed to be accepting the fact that she was growing up, and at that moment, Tess couldn't imagine why anyone would want to be anything other than human.

'We'll still have to look for him, of course,' she said. 'He's going to need a bit of support for a while.'

'We can leave the sharpened stake at home, though,' said Kevin. 'Do you think we should go now?'

Tess shook her head. 'I'm done in. This evening, maybe. The only thing I want to do now is to sleep all day.'

Kevin nodded. 'Good idea.' He stood up and stretched, then set off for the spare room. At the door he turned back, grinning widely.

'Just promise me you won't make a habit of it,' he said.

KATE THOMPSON

THE *Switchers* TRILOGY

'**Kate Thompson writes with a marvellous and magical ease.**' TES

Kate Thompson's Switchers trilogy is riveting reading. Once you have begun, you will never want to stop.

Switchers

Tess is a Switcher - she can change shape to become any animal she chooses. She always thought she was unique, but not any more. Tess meets another Switcher, Kevin, and together they have powers they never dreamed of.

Midnight's Choice *Switchers 2*

Tess senses a call which is at once welcoming and terrifying, too. Will she choose the path of darkness…?

Wild Blood *Switchers 3*

With her fifteenth birthday imminent, Tess is running out of time to decide who, or what, she will become when she switches for the last time. What on earth will she do in the wilds of the woods? And what will the wild woods do to her?

OUT NOW IN PAPERBACK FROM RED FOX AT £4.99

the BEGUILERS

KATE THOMPSON

'You calm down, young lady,
or it's off after beguilers
you'll be.' Maybe my mother
shouldn't have said that.
Maybe it put the idea into
my head.

Every night they came drifting through the village
streets, issuing their mournful cries, terrorizing the
population. It wasn't safe to go out after dark.
Everyone knew the power of the beguilers.

No one knew what they were. No one had ever caught
one. But every generation threw up a beguiler hunter;
a tragic soul considered by the rest of the villagers
to be insane.

Rilka knows she isn't mad. But the desire to catch a
beguiler is about to change her life, and the lives of
those around her, for ever.

Out now in Hardback from The Bodley Head.
ISBN 0370325737   £10.99

ONLY HUMAN

Kate Thompson

The second book in The Missing Link trilogy

Whatever it was that had caught him was heading straight down for the deep. Although he didn't have a dolphin's sonar system, Danny had a strong sixth sense that helped him to orient himself in the darkness of the sea and identify other living things. He had encountered all sorts of weird and wonderful creatures in the deep, but the one that was dragging him now was something outside his experience.

About a hundred metres down, Danny's captor levelled off and began to swim parallel to the surface, away from *The Privateer*. Now Danny could feel the powerful beating of fins creating turbulence in the water beside his head. His panic was depriving him of oxygen, and he began to fear that he would drown before this creature, whatever it was, ever got around to eating him. With a tremendous effort, he bent double and managed to reach his ankle. But what his fingers encountered there sent a swift shock through his blood.

There was no mouth, no teeth, no predator's jaw. The thing that gripped him felt much more like a human hand.

Now available from The Bodley Head at £10.99
ISBN 0370326636